AMERICAN FABLES
for the
Politically Incorrect

by Carl Charbonnet

Dust jacket art and illustrations by: Jeff Gregory

American de Tocqueville Press
P.O. Box 130088
Birmingham, Alabama 35213 U. S. A.

This book is fiction. The type of fiction is satire with good doses of irony and allegory thrown in.

Most of the names were pulled out of the air. For those names there was no intent to identify real people. Some names are of real people. All the real people are, or were when living, famous persons.

American de Tocqueville Press,
P.O. Box 130088
Birmingham, Alabama 35213 U. S. A.

Printed in the United States of America
First printing November 1995

Charbonnet, Carl
  American Fables for the Politically Incorrect / Carl Charbonnet
  ISBN 0-9648786-0-7
  1. Humor. 2 Fables, modern. 3 Satire, Political.
  4 Philosophy, Political. 5 Philosophy, moral.

Dedication

The Constitution is the basis for our nation's rule of law. It is the world's best protection against the rule of men. It decrees limited government. It is an impediment to all forms of leftism - not just Liberalism (the word Americans use today for socialism), but Nazism and Communism as well.

The dominant media and "educational" community usually act as though they believe and support the Constitution, but in truth they despise it. They try to ignore those who do believe in the Constitution and when that becomes difficult they harass and vilify them without kindness.

The main purpose of the Constitution is to protect Americans from the United States government. The Constitution limits the government to a very few rights, which are enumerated. It specifically prohibits the government from attempting either to hurt or to help the American people except in the few, limited and enumerated areas.

This book is dedicated to that tiny minority of men and women who understand, believe in and stand up for the Constitution.

Acknowledgments

First to God, who created me and sustains me.

Then to Western Civilization, the best attempt in all history of a free and just society by a country mile.

Then to the land of my birth, America – built on a foundation of:

1. Judeo-Christianity,
2. The spirit of freedom, self reliance and charity,
3. and a Constitution which allows freedom because it restricts government to a few enumerated roles - but is now threatened from within by those who believe our government can and should solve our problems in a never ending and ever increasing intervention.

Then to Louise Antoinette Hellmers Charbonnet and Wilfred James Charbonnet, who by my incredible good fortune were my parents and who transferred God's love to me overflowing my cup.

And to the following people for their specific help on my epic novel *Sadistic Intent* (not yet published) and *American Fables for the Politically Incorrect*: Marjorie Swanson; Kitty Ramsay; John Ramsay, Jr.; Don Collins, who encouraged and inspired me and has now left us; Hannah Collins; Denice George; Hank Grey; June and Jack Cunniff; Anne Nall Stallworth; Dr. Ronald L. Trowbridge; Libby Hughes; Kathy Miller; James. E. Jacobson; John MacLeod, who always showed interest in the book and has now left us; Cheryl Buck; Steve Coleman, Jr.; John C. Bird; John T. Bird; Malcolm Steve Forbes, Jr.; Jacques Alfred Charbonnet,

American Fables for the Politically Incorrect

from whose Civil War Diary I borrowed what I judge to be the most beautiful sentence in Sadistic Intent; Killian Loew Charbonnet from whom I borrowed a clever sentence; Yevonne Chapell; John F McManus; Jimmy Copeland; Evelyn Stough; Dan McKeever; Billy Guin; Erwin Glikes, the only book editor of a big publishing company I was able to find who thought Reagan was a better President than Clinton is, and who believed in the limited government decreed by the Constitution (I aspired to become his close friend when he died at 56 while organizing his own imprint at PENGUIN GROUP); Bobby Frese; Dr. Clarence Carson, whose many books every literate American should read; Myrtice Carson, whose kind interest propelled me; Professor Paul Cleveland; William Christian Charbonnet, my son and second severest critic who exhorted me to make my points with subtlety; Charles Chigna Andy Kilpatrick; Mary Nash; Nelson Nash; Lisa Bricker Mosley; Mark Meares, who always remembered; Harold See; Robert Norman, Sr.; James C. Barton, Sr.; Martha Carolyn Edwards; Jim Smith, grandson of Elna Smith, grandnephew of Edmund Opitz; Edmund Opitz; Dr. Richard D. Glasow; Hans F. Sennholz; Jim and Cookie Kidd; Professor Mark LaGory; Mary Lou Yeilding; Sue Charbonnet; James & Kitty Sutherland; Ed Richner; H. Kneel Ball; Norma McKittrick super copy chief; Tom Bailey, Douglas E. Dutton, Chip and Martha Grizzle, Holly Barnard, Jim Smith of Litho Plate & Negative, Bill Cather of Cather Publishing, Margaret (Skip) Laneyand especially Rosemary Chambers, who, after my friend and inspiration Don Collins died, came from nowhere to take up the baton and fill me with encouragement.

"America is great because America is good. If she ceases to be good she will cease to be great."

Alexis de Tocqueville, 1835

Contents

I	San Francisco:	
	The City That Could Have Been	1
II	Nutrition	9
III	The So What, Who Cares Hedonist	13
IV	The Ants and the Grasshopper	23
V	Propaganda	33
VI	The Prophet	35
VII	Margi's Problem	47
VIII	The Good Abortionist	59
IX	Morality Cannot be Legislated	61
X	Arms	73
XI	Diogenes	81
XII	Art	109
XIII	The Water Shortage	113
XIV	Adie	117
XV	Woodpecker	123
XVI	The Pilgrims	129
XVII	Quality of Life	133
XVIII	The Invention of Language	149
XIX	Robbers	157
XX	Tabloids at the Check-Out Counter	171
XXI	Promises, Promises	175

American Fables for the Politically Incorrect

List of Illustrations

The Unbiased Journalist	32
The Good Abortionist	58
Diogenes	80
The First Word	148

Preface

Consider reading these stories one at a time.

Discuss each one with your husband, your wife, a neighbor, a friend. Read another story the next day.

You might want to use them to stimulate a discussion group.

But most of all, enjoy them.

AMERICAN FABLES
for the
Politically Incorrect

SAN FRANCISCO:
THE CITY THAT COULD HAVE BEEN

It was hard for Professor Kirksen to hide the feeling of humiliation as he was forced to teach a class of undergraduates at prestigious Bovundy University. It was the first undergraduate class he had taught in five years. After all, wasn't he the renowned Dr. Kirksen, author of fifteen books and ninety-nine research papers? Hadn't he been a full professor at the nation's best university for twenty years? Wasn't he one of the nation's leading intellectuals?

It was with peevish disdain that he had taught the class for three weeks laying what he considered a basic foundation in political science.

Today he began, "These last three weeks I have tried to impress upon you the necessity of the federal government in Washington to plan, control and direct our lives. You should now know that without the help of the federal government, there would be regression, chaos and famine.

"As we speak, our benevolent federal government is sending massive aid to the flood victims in the Midwest. In 1992 Hurricane Andrew devastated South Florida, destroying tens of thousands of homes. Federal help put people back on their feet. That same year the twin evils of racism and capitalism caused a justified reaction as Los Angeles rioted. Six hundred buildings were burned and fifty-two citizens were killed. The federal government came to the aid of Los Angeles with loans and outright grants. Los Angeles will survive.

"In 1964 a massive earthquake hit Alaska. Seventy thousand square miles of land rose. Several cities were devastated, and their infrastructures were destroyed. Washington came through, giving aid to the State, cities and individuals. Alaska was saved.

"But perhaps you do not know that in the primitive days of our country the United States government did not help as it does today. Yes, that's right. There was a time when the government in Washington cared so little for the people of the United States that they did not lift a finger to help.

"For example, let me tell you about a beautiful city nestled between the bay and the ocean. It was called San Francisco, California on the Pacific Ocean, about 400 miles north of Los Angeles. At the turn of the

San Francisco, The City That Could Have Been

century San Francisco was a bustling, booming city. Then on April 18th, 1906, a great earthquake struck. San Francisco was immensely damaged. Gas mains ruptured and fires raged out of control for three days. What had not been destroyed by the shaking earth was destroyed by fire. And the federal government did nothing. That is why there is no San Francisco today for us to enjoy."

A student raised his hand.

"Yes, Mr. Borders, you have a question?"

"Sir, last summer I visited San Francisco. It's still there."

Professor Kirksen scowled. *The impudence of students today,* he thought. *Not only do I have to teach these children but I have to put up with their impertinence also.* Then he spoke as though to a four-year-old, "Mr. Borders, there are many beautiful cities on the California coast, Carmel, Sausalito and others. California has many cities that begin with 'San.' I'm sure what you saw was one of those."

"No sir, it was San Francisco."

The professor's neck grew red with anger, "Mr. Borders, I want to talk with you after class."

~~~~~~~~~~~~~~~~~~~~~~~~~~

At the completion of class Professor Kirksen strode out the room with Borders following. Neither said a word. The Professor turned left into a room with a long table and took a seat. No one spoke.

One by one three teaching assistants walked in and silently took seats.

Then the great professor spoke to the three assistants, "Mr. Borders spoke up in class today, saying he had visited San Francisco."

The first assistant spoke, "There have been seven archaeological reports on the area. I have read them. Some archaeologists traveled the eastern shore of the bay to reach the ruins; some took the coastal route. The reports are all the same: a few primitive people staring blankly with fear from behind dusty ruins." Then looking straight at Borders, "Is that what you found?"

"Oh, no sir. It is a regular city with crowded streets and busy people everywhere. We went to Fisherman's Wharf and had steamed clams and fried crab claws."

Professor Kirksen looked at the first assistant as if to say, *Now do you see what I mean!*

"How long have you been in Professor Border's class?"

"Three weeks."

"And what did he cover?"

"The place government plays in America."

"And what place does the government play in America?"

"According to Professor Kirksen the government plans, organizes and controls our lives." The Professor did not miss the, 'According to Professor Kirksen.'

"And without the government in Washington, what would happen?"

"He said we would degrade to chaos and famine."

The second assistant asked, "Why do you think you visited San Francisco?"

Sometimes when an answer is so obvious, it is difficult to find words of explanation. Borders stammered and then said, "My father said we were going to San Francisco. We drove a long time and then entered the city. We stayed three days - my father, my mother and my three sisters."

"What does your father do?"

"He owns a small string of specialty shops in Utah and Wyoming."

That brought some relief for the Professor and the three teaching assistants. One assistant said, "Then he's a businessman. That explains a good deal."

Then the professor spoke, "Now let's look at the facts: First, in 1906 a great earthquake devastated San Francisco; second, it is necessary in such situations for the government to send aid to save such a devastated city; third, the federal government did nothing to help. The conclusion is inescapable: San Francisco did not survive. Today there is no San Francisco as there was at the turn of the century."

The third assistant spoke up, "I spent two years under the supervision of Professor Kirksen while I worked on my Ph.D. I have read all fifteen of his books and more than forty of his excellent papers. I have read papers and books of other leading intellectuals and now have my own Ph.D. I have been privileged. You are privileged, Mr. Borders. You are at Bovundy University. That means you are one of the select. You have been chosen for an education. Education means that you know. Verification is not necessary when one knows. We are not empirical here - we are educated. We are not interested in what you think you did last summer because we know you did not visit San Francisco because we know there is no San Francisco to visit. Being educated we know the opinions, prejudices and motives of reactionaries. It is a waste of time to bother with them because we know them. We know they have nothing to say. As Professor Kirksen has told you, San Francisco was destroyed by an earthquake in 1906, the federal government did not send aid, therefore there is no San Francisco for you to visit.

"Do you understand it now, Mr. Borders?"

"Well, er ..."

The first assistant irritably broke in, "It's easy to see why so many students come to us unprepared. We have to teach remedial classes. And it is easiest of all to understand you, Mr. Borders. You admit your father is a businessman. I'm sure he has filled your mind with prejudices. You probably didn't even go to a public kindergarten or primary school. You are so

San Francisco, The City That Could Have Been

biased that even as we carefully explain what had to
have happened you still do not get it. Are you aware
that you are today endangering your career?"

"Why ..."

In a more intimidating and louder voice the second
assistant leaned closer and added, "Instead of being
grateful for being at a top university, you are harassing
Professor Kirksen who has been very charitably deal-
ing with you, I might point out. Someone of his
stature should not be subject to your impertinence. Do
you really think you know more than Professor
Kirksen?"

"I, er ..."

"Gentlemen," said the great Professor in his most sug-
ary voice, "young Borders is trying. It takes time.
Let's give him a chance."

~~~~~~~~~~~~~~~~~~~~~~~~~~~

Students filed into the room at the next class meeting. Professor Kirksen surveyed the students with
confidence before speaking.

"At our last meeting," he chuckled, "Mr. Borders
told us he had visited San Francisco with his family
last summer.

"Mr. Borders, what do you have to say today?"

The student rose, stood with his head down, then
said in a faint voice, "It must have been Sausalito that
we visited."

NUTRITION

The meeting began well enough. After all, Dr. Oglethorpe was well-known and respected.

He was not as famous as Petar the hockey player, but for a scientist his fame was absolute among his peers - and considerable among the rest of us. I mean, who could name even one biological scientist? Not many. But almost everybody had heard of Dr. Oglethorpe. Everybody knew nutritional science began in the 20th century and was today, two hundred years later, one of the most important of the sciences. People could relate to it.

So facing a respectful, attentive audience, Dr. Oglethorpe began his talk on the progress of nutritional science to the joint session of Congress. The Cabinet and members of the Supreme Court were there too.

Now that is how things started, but soon it became hard for me to pay attention. Then I knew the good

Carl Charbonnet

doctor was really in trouble when the guy next to me
fell asleep. You know, it wasn't like he was saying
things we could understand. He was talking about
tetons and betons without telling us what those things
were. *Are they like raisins?* I wondered as I fidgeted
in my chair. *Did my wife, Elaine, forget my size and
buy my shorts too small or am I gaining weight? How
can a guy get comfortable when his shorts have crept
up and made him uncomfortable? If we were all men
I could reach down and readjust them, but there are
women here too. Let's see, the nearest woman is two
chairs to the right. Maybe I can unzip real fast, reach
down, readjust them quickly, zip up again and she
won't notice.*

A guy four rows ahead was snoring so loudly that a
man came from somewhere down the aisle and
motioned for his seatmate to quiet him down.

The great Oglethorpe continued.

I could see the face of President Hollister seated
high on the podium. It was consternation I saw.
Finally the President interrupted the doctor's speech,
"Dr. Oglethorpe, we are not scientists. I was wonder-
ing if you could tell us in lay terms what you have
been saying in scientific terms."

Well, the doctor didn't like anybody criticizing
him, not even the President of the United States. He
looked at the President and said, "Harrumph." I didn't
think people said harrumph anymore, but he did. I
heard him, it was harrumph. So the doctor droned on

Nutrition

much as before and by this time I could see other men squirming in their seats and wondered if there had recently been a sale of undersized men's shorts.

One woman was shaking her watch, a man six seats away nodded and three men on my right squirmed. When I saw the President staring at the door, I twisted my head around and looked. Three Congressmen were beseeching the guards to let them leave. That's all the President needed.

He slammed his gavel, "Dr. Oglethorpe, every man and every woman in this chamber appreciates the great work you have done on nutritional science. All of us and our children are leading more healthful and vigorous lives because of your important work. But this meeting has gone on long enough. Will you please summarize for us, in one sentence, the essence of good nutrition so I may adjourn this joint session of Congress."

Blood ran up Dr. Oglethorpe's neck and reddened his face. He sputtered and fumed and then said, "All right, if you want my ten years of research into the two Centuries of Progress boiled down to one sentence, I will give it to you."

The doctor got control of himself. He grabbed the lectern with both hands. He lifted his head and looked from side to side until everyone was quiet. When he was sure he had everyone's attention he said –

"An apple a day keeps the doctor away."

THE SO WHAT,
WHO CARES HEDONIST

Ronald Sessions was lying on the sofa with his knees up and a closed book on his stomach. He tapped the book with his fingers to the rhythm of loud music from his record player.

His father rose, walked to the record player and turned the volume down, "Your Aunt Shirley is coming for dinner and you're rumpled and wearing a dirty shirt."

"So what?"

"She'll feel better if you were neat looking."

"Who cares?"

"I care and you should too."

"All right," said Ronald, "I'll put on a clean shirt."

As Ronald began walking upstairs his father said, "And consider taking a bath and shaving while you're at it."

"All right, Dad. I'll clean up."

~~~~~~~~~~~~~~~~~~~~~~~~~

When the door chimes rang Ronald jumped up, walked to the door and opened it, "Aunt Shirley, come in. It's so good to see you. Did that mysterious man ever call you back?"

"Never mind about him. You look nice, Ronald. Is that a new shirt?"

"It is. Put it on just for you."

"Thank you, Ronald.

"Walter, you look tired. How is business?"

"It's a burden, but I'm surviving. I had hoped Ronald would join the firm. That would have been a big help."

"Ronald, why don't you start working?" asked Aunt Shirley.

"It's the war, you know."

"World War II has been over for six years. Your father used his influence to get you a commission as a 2nd Lieutenant. You never did tell me your war experiences. Do you want to tell me now?"

"What's there to tell when you're in the Quartermaster Corps?"

"The Quartermaster Corps is important or the Army wouldn't have it," responded Aunt Shirley. "I was so proud of you. It seemed like every time I talked with your father, you had a new promotion.

The So What, Who Cares Hedonist

You made it all the way to Lt. Colonel. Now it seems time for you to go to work again."
"Why work? Dad is rich. He supports me."

~~~~~~~~~~~~~~~~~~~~~~~~~~~~

The stroke was massive; suffering was brief. Some say Ronald Sessions' father worked himself to death, staying in his office until way past dark and then bringing more work home with him in his briefcase.

Ronald was shocked to learn that his inheritance was sufficient to support him for only one year. What was he to do?

A friend urged him to run for the Senate.

"But I have no experience."

"You've got the best experience you could have at this time, you are a war hero."

"I am? I didn't know that."

"Better than that, you're a humble war hero. With your personality you can beat the opposition."

~~~~~~~~~~~~~~~~~~~~~~~~~~~~

As a Senator Ronald never read a bill. He seldom voted on the floor.

He learned that as a United States Senator he was a big shot. People greeted him in the street. In restaurants he was asked for autographs. He noticed that women smiled at him more, stood closer to him,

Carl Charbonnet

squeezed notes into his hand.

He had kept Harry Cordoner, who had managed his predecessor's office, and let him run his office. In three years the most urgent meeting he ever had with his staff began one Tuesday morning after a strenuous weekend of partying. "I have a problem," he began. "My Senator's salary is not enough to keep up my lifestyle. What can be done?"

A thoughtful Harry Cordoner replied, "Your biggest expenses are your extravagant parties. I'll find a way to put them on your expense account."

His favorite parties featured beautiful young women.

He also enjoyed giving parties for other Senators. He would listen to their ideas and respond with charming blandness or sometimes a clever, inoffensive joke. There was no more popular politician in Washington than Senator Sessions.

At the presidential convention the two leading candidates were locked in a battle for the nomination. Neither could get a majority. Their supporters were polarized and adamant. After the forty-sixth ballot, a caucus was convened. Both sides agreed to drop out in favor of Ronald Sessions if he would agree to run. Ronald was nominated on the forty-seventh ballot.

In the general election his nonchalant, uncaring attitude was viewed as being above the dirty politics of many other candidates of the day. He was elected with a comfortable margin.

The So What, Who Cares Hedonist

~~~~~~~~~~~~~~~~~~~~~~~~~~~~

If being a Senator had been fun, being the President was even better. If women had been attracted to a Senator, they were more attracted to the President. Ronald Sessions enjoyed being president.

His advisors told him what he absolutely had to do. Otherwise he did nothing as far as the government was concerned. Air Force One went back and forth between the Caribbean, the French Riviera and Las Vegas. He didn't go alone; always there were beautiful women, and often his men friends, both in and out of politics. He was out of the country most of the time.

At that time it was the law in the United States that no bill could become law without the President's signature. Existing laws expired unless renewed. For the first two years virtually no legislation was passed in our nation's capital. Existing laws expired. Every month fewer national laws governed the country. The number of pages in the Congressional Register was reduced by two-thirds.

As the government receded, the cracks and crevices between the laws grew larger. This left the people with more freedom to create, to grow, to prosper, to live. Family ties became stronger. Life made more sense so morality expanded.

Meanwhile state and local governments continued to punish crime, record deeds and adjudicate disputes.

Crime throughout the nation decreased each year.

Carl Charbonnet

The world watched as, unexpectedly, the economy increased at unheard of rates. A leading economist said, "Our government is handicapped with an inactive President. This 12% increase in the Gross National Product is an aberration and cannot continue. We must get the attention of the president and have him sign these important bills before the crash comes." The economy increased the next year at 13%.

President Sessions was reelected by a landslide.

But something had to be done. Intellectual journals wrote of the horrors of a weak government crippled by an absent President. Someone had to talk sense into President Sessions. But no one knew where the President was.

Eventually he was recognized on a yacht cruising the South China Sea. The yacht was large enough to hold the crew, Secret Service men, three pals and eight young women. The yacht was 700 miles out of Hong Kong, north of the Philippines and on the way to the Marianas when a U.S. Navy cruiser approached it and came alongside. High above the yacht, at the railing of the great ship, stood a young officer in a beautiful white uniform. He shouted through a megaphone, "Permission to board is requested."

"Ask him how many people," said the President.

"How many people?" his assistant shouted.

"One, sir," the officer shouted.

"One, sir," his assistant said.

The So What, Who Cares Hedonist

"Let 'um come," said the President.

"Permission to board is granted," the assistant shouted.

An impeccably dressed civilian, about sixty years old, held the railing with one hand and a briefcase with the other as he overcame the bouncing sea and made it to the deck of the yacht.

"Mr. President, you're looking fit," said the visitor as his eyes followed the swaying Ronald Sessions.

"And who are you?" asked the President.

"I'm Secretary of State Osborn, Mr. President. Don't you remember? You appointed me."

"Oh yes, if you say so.

"You have a first name, Osborn?"

"David."

"Ginger, this is David Osborn, Ginger ... Ginger ..."

"McIntire."

"This is Ginger McIntire. What you drinking, Osborn?"

"I have important matters to discuss. May we retire to the privacy of your cabin?"

"Ginger, where is Pauline? Get her over here for Osborn. He looks like he could use a woman. Osborn, wait until you see Pauline. You'll forget why you're here. And she's a good sport."

A trim young woman with flowing hair, wearing a halter top and shorts, came over and took the Secretary's arm. "I'm Pauline."

"How do you do. I'm Secretary of State Osborn.

"Mr. President, a joint resolution of Congress requested that I visit you. May we go to your cabin for privacy?"

"No. If you have something to say, say it to all of us. Pauline's smart. Maybe she can make a contribution."

"Very well. If that's the way it must be."

"Mr. President, the country is suffering. No new laws are being passed. The opposition has set up gridlock for every proposed law and you are not there to lead us and to sign the laws."

"So what?"

"So what? We need to pass laws. That's what government is for, to pass laws. We are the laughing stock of governments all over the world. They are solving problems, passing laws and we are not."

"Mr. Secretary," said Pauline, "I'm sure Ronnie would like to help, but let me tell you something. In every country we go to, people ask me personally to help them get permission to emigrate to the United States. Maybe we don't need so many laws."

The Secretary of State turned to Pauline. He looked at her from her bare feet to her tousled hair then said, "You don't look to me like someone who has a graduate degree in government from Harvard."

Then turning his attention back to the President he said, "Now Mr. President, if we can't have a discussion, at least grant this request. The best and the brightest have developed 158 proposals for new regu-

The So What, Who Cares Hedonist

lations, mandates, programs to help the needy and tax increases. Twenty-seven have been passed by the Congress and await your signature. I have with me in my briefcase the three most important. This is urgent. I need you to sign these three bills. The country needs you to sign these bills. The government is in shambles and will continue to be if you don't sign them."

"So what?"

"But Mr. President, your country needs you."

"Who cares?"

The Secretary's mouth fell open as the President lifted a bottle of whiskey to his mouth, drank the remaining contents, and passed out. Secretary of State Osborn returned to the Navy ship without achieving his mission.

~~~~~~~~~~~~~~~~~~~~~~~~~~~

Meanwhile, back in the United States peace reigned and prosperity soared. The economy continued to break records. Professors and journalists throughout the world wrote circuitous essays purporting to explain the anomaly between the impotent government and the bountiful society.

THE ANTS AND
THE GRASSHOPPER

The leaves in the tops of the trees rustled in the wind. The sun shone on the tall grass of the meadow stretching between the trees. On the quiet meadow floor, where the grass touched the ground, out of sight of the deer and the bears, ants were busy.

They ran forward, they ran to the left, they ran to the right, they ran in circles – they were looking for food. One ant found an aphid, another a leaf segment, while the third held a seed in her mouth. As soon as one found an aphid, another a leaf segment and the third a seed, each ant returned to the trail and together in a long, thin line they carried the food back to their house. As they headed home they passed other ants racing out to forage for more food.

The ants made thousands of trips from the meadow to the ant home. All autumn the ants worked.

One day as they worked they saw the grasshopper singing and jumping about.

"Mr. Grasshopper," said one of the ants. "Winter will be here soon. Have you put away a store of food for the winter?"

"Oh, no. Of course not."

"When the cold winds of winter come it will be too late. Why don't you gather food for the winter?"

"I would rather play."

So the ants went on with their work until their home held enough food to last through a long winter.

And the winter did come. The wind blew and the snow flew and the ants were cozy and warm inside their home.

One day they heard a knocking. Fearful of opening the door to the cruel winter, one ant opened the peephole in the big door. She saw the grasshopper holding both his top arms around his chest in a vain effort to keep warm.

"What do you want?" asked the ant.

"I want food. I'm starving," said the grasshopper.

"We told you to store up food, but you said you would rather play. Now you must be responsible for your own conduct. Go away."

The ant closed the peephole just as she heard the grasshopper shout, "You'll be sorry for this!"

The grasshopper went directly to the poverty law center and spoke to a plaintiff's attorney whose salary

The Ants and The Grasshopper

was paid by the government in Washington. "Sir, I am hungry. The ants have lots of food but they will not give me any."

"We'll see about that," said the plaintiff's attorney. "I'll get a warrant and we'll search the place to see if they are hoarding food."

The next day the plaintiff's attorney waving a warrant, the grasshopper and six deputies walked through the snow to the ant home. The plaintiff's attorney knocked loudly.

One of the ants opened the peephole and saw the sardonic, grinning face of the plaintiff's attorney. "What do you want?" she asked.

"I want to come in."

"Why would I want to let in a plaintiff's attorney with a sardonic, grinning face?"

"You will want to let me in because I have the force of the government behind me."

The ant looked more intently through the peephole and saw the grasshopper and the six deputies. She was perplexed, *Should I let them in or should I stand up for my rights and keep the door shut and locked?* "Just a minute," she said.

She turned to her fellow ants, "This is serious. There is a plaintiff's attorney at the door with a warrant, the grasshopper and six deputies. They have the force of government on their side, and they want to come in. What shall we do?"

Carl Charbonnet

"We have right on our side," said one.

"Do the deputies have guns?" asked another.

"Let me look," said the first ant as she reopened the peephole and looked. She shut the peephole, turned around and said, "Yes."

"I say, let's not let them in," said a fourth.

Then they all said, "Let's not let them in. This is our home and our home is our castle."

So the first ant opened the peephole and told the plaintiff's attorney, "We talked it over and decided that this is our home, our castle. We did nothing wrong; we will not let you in. Go away."

The plaintiff's attorney's sardonic grin changed to a vicious snarl as he turned to the deputies, giving orders.

Meanwhile, inside the warm cozy house, the ants sat down to a convivial dinner. "I think this is going to be a real cold winter," said one.

"Not as cold as the winter of '78," said a second.

"Well, that was the coldest ever. It can still be very cold yet not that cold," the first ant replied.

They heard a strange noise. Then a bumping. As the bumping grew louder, they realized that something very big and powerful was pounding on their door from the outside.

The first ant started to walk to the door to see what was happening, but before she reached it, the loudest bump of all shook the house as the door was ripped from its hinges. It came crashing into the room and

The Ants and The Grasshopper

slid across the floor.

In rushed the cold winter air, the grasshopper, a fanatic waving a warrant and six deputies. "Look everywhere," said the grasshopper as he turned to sneer at the ants.

The deputies scurried this way and that, up and down, opening every door, entering every room and closet until one said loudly and with pride, "Here it is. I found it."

Quietness overcame them as they walked to gaze through the opened door into a large room filled high with aphids, leaf segments and seeds.

The chief deputy majestically walked to the ants still sitting at their dinner table. He spread his feet apart, put his left hand on his hip then spoke, "You have the right to remain silent. Anything you say may be used against you. You have the right to have an attorney present when questioned. If you cannot afford an attorney, one will be appointed. Do you understand this?"

"Huh?"

"We're confiscating this contraband."

"Contraband?" wondered the first ant. "We have furniture, a few clothes, some tools and enough food to last the winter. But we don't have any contraband."

"There, you just admitted it: enough food to last the winter. Don't you know that's hoarding, and hoarding is an evil capitalistic conspiracy based on greed."

The plaintiff's attorney standing at the chief

deputy's side moved his long tongue across his lips and rubbed his slender fingers together.

The chief deputy turned toward the door opening and said, "Okay, bring it in." A smoking, noisy, very small front-end loader entered the ants' home, drove to the storeroom and scooped up a load of dry seeds. It backed up and out of the house to deposit the load in a large truck and then returned for another load. It continued back and forth from storeroom to truck.

"But you're taking our food!" exclaimed the first ant. "We'll starve without our food."

"The government will take care of you."

As the front-end loader passed with a load of seeds, the hungry grasshopper reached in the bucket and took a handful. Before he could put it in his mouth, one of the deputies whacked him on the wrist with his pistol, knocking the seeds to the floor. "That property is under the jurisdiction of the government. Keep your hands out of it."

So hungry was the grasshopper that he bent down, picked up a seed that had fallen to the floor and quickly put it in his mouth. As he reached for a second seed the deputy put his hobnailed boot on the grasshopper's hand. "I told you to keep away from that property. Don't you know the law!"

It had taken the ants more than six weeks to harvest and store their food: the deputies removed it in less than six hours. Then they handcuffed the hoarders.

The Ants and The Grasshopper

Since this was a Federal case, they also put each ant in leg irons. The fact that installing leg irons, for ants accused of a white collar crime, was cruel and unusual punishment did not bother the officers. They then took them away.

"When can I get some of the food?" asked the weakening grasshopper.

"Go to the welfare office and fill out the proper form."

Dutifully the grasshopper went from office to office until he found the right office. He sat in a chair and wearily filled out the form. He handed it to the clerk who said, "We'll be in contact with you after the form is processed."

"Three weeks later the grasshopper's phone rang. He was so weak now that he could barely lift the phone, "Hello."

"Mr. Grasshopper?"

"Yes, I'm Mr. Grasshopper."

"Mr. Grasshopper, you filled out form 1933-A. That's not the form for obtaining dry seed that has been confiscated from hoarders. It's for obtaining dry, fresh seed that the government has purchased from farmers to get their vote. You should have filled out form 1933-B. You must come in and fill out the proper form."

It took all his strength to answer, "I'll try."

A winter snow was lightly falling. Mr. Grasshopper

Carl Charbonnet

headed for the welfare office. He hopped, or tried to hop, but he was too weak. He began to crawl. Then, as his strength left him he crawled more slowly. Then he stopped crawling. Snow began to cover his body.

The next morning when two deputies were walking to work they saw the carcass of the grasshopper. As they stepped around it one said, "We do our job. Why can't the street department workers keep our streets clean?"

THE UNBIASED JOURNALIST

PROPAGANDA

Today the dominant media are trying to convince us that Justice Clarence Thomas is a crude person, like President Bill and Hillary Clinton are.

And they are trying to convince us that Bill and Hillary Clinton are nice people, like Clarence Thomas is.

THE PROPHET

Five men sat and talked in the general store that day, four farmers and the proprietor.

The farmers were used to working in the fields behind mules or with hoes from sunup to sundown. Their wives worked longer than that in the house putting up vegetables, baking bread, churning butter, making clothes and keeping the house clean. Their children worked too. The boys helped their fathers in the field and the girls helped their mothers in the house.

Once a month they came to Ezra's store to buy salt, sugar, flour and sometimes tools, rough cloth or seeds. They arranged to come the same day to visit each other and relax a little. Caleb and Warren had come in wagons. John had ridden his mule. Clyde had walked, as it was only four miles from his farm and his son was using his mule.

It was 1792. The War for Independence had ended

Carl Charbonnet

eleven years ago at Yorktown. They had lived five years under the new Constitution. Some people were leaving the tidelands to carve out new lives in the western wilderness.

It was November in Virginia. An early cold wind was blowing and whistling through the cracks in Ezra's country store. Four men were crowded in front of the stone fireplace talking crops and mules and how hard it was to survive. Even as they complained their pride showed through as they described the hardships they had overcome. "It's a rough life," said John, "but a good one. Elenor is a good woman and I'm a fortunate man to have her as my wife."

Ezra, the proprietor, was cutting strips of beef and salting them when the rattling of the door got his attention. He looked up to see an old man silhouetted by the open door.

"Howdy, friends. May I join you?"

"Sure," said Caleb.

"You're welcome, stranger," said Ezra.

The old man removed the bundle from his back and looked around for a place to put it. "Just put it on the floor next to them barrels," said Ezra.

"Come get warm," said Warren, as he and the others made room for him.

"Thank you, sirs." He moved up to the fire and rubbed his hands.

Clyde couldn't keep his curiosity to himself. "Where you from, stranger?"

The Prophet

"I've been down in North Carolina and before that, Georgia. Before that I was in Europe for a while."

"You searching for family or something?" Clyde asked.

"No, just walking, observing and talking. Sometimes I write."

"You walk mighty straight and proud for an old man."

"Thank you, sir, for I am old. I'm eighty-two. I thank God I can still walk and talk. I do lots of talking and would like to say something to you now."

"Go on."

"I'm hungry. I didn't know there were so few towns out west. I ran out of food two days ago. It's too late in the year for berries and I'm very hungry. I'll trade you tales and prophecies for food."

The men looked at each other not knowing what to do or say, at first,. But the manner and appearance of the old man evoked respect and encouraged them.

"I'll chip in," said Caleb as he put down two pennies on a box.

Warren took potatoes from his sack and put them on the box. John cut a piece of cheese for his contribution. Clyde cut a loaf of brown bread in half and placed one part on the box. John put down two pennies. "I'll give you corn cakes and jerky to take with you when you leave," said Ezra.

"Thank you all, you've very generous," said the stranger as he unsheathed a knife from a scabbard on his waist and cut a piece of cheese and a slice of bread.

Carl Charbonnet

He put the piece of cheese on the bread and ate in silence as the others watched.

When finished he took the pennies and put them in a pouch tied to his waist. He put the larger items on the floor beside his bundle. He stood up and looked at them, "I'm ready now, if you are, for my stories and prophecies."

Caleb got up and offered his box for the old man to sit on. He sat down and began:

"Wonderful things are happening.

"Our new United States is prospering and growing. The European countries are prospering too. In England and Scotland they are experimenting with fiery engines that do the work of horses and mules. In a few years these engines will be put into great carriages called locomotives that will pull several other carriages on rails of iron. In France never before seen looms are being built that make beautiful and strong cloth at a price so low that everyone in this store would be able to buy clothes made from it. In Italy and Austria new music has already been composed and performed, raising art to a new high level. During the next century, the nineteenth century, more great music will be composed in Europe than has so far been composed in all countries in all history.

"And this is the gist of what I shall prophesy for you: In a country as free as our United States, progress will pile upon progress. In the nineteenth century the United States will become a powerful country and will begin to take over the lead in science and invention from Europe. In the twentieth century we will be the most prosperous and powerful country in the world.

"Two hundreds years from today, businesses will have produced such wonders that have not yet become dreams.

"You will have in your home a voice connector so that you can talk with your neighbor."

"My closest neighbor is seven miles," said John.

"You will be able to talk with him and also your brother in Richmond."

All the men leaned forward to catch every word.

"You will have in your home, sound machines, that will bring sound from far away - music and news and stories for entertainment. That's not the end of it. By 1992 you will have picture machines in your home that will bring you moving pictures of things as they happen in other cities, and plays and singing as well."

"How are we going to buy these wonderful things?" asked Warren.

"Each marvelous thing that business produces increases the wealth of all. As the years go by we will have more money to spend. Buying food and other necessities will not be a problem, as we will have money left over for luxuries.

"Water will be delivered to your home in underground pipes. Pipes inside your house will deliver the water where you want it, and you will be able to select hot or cold water."

"Hot or cold water!"

"It will be good for drinking and so cheap you will be able to wash your automobile."

"What's an automobile?" asked Clyde.

"An automobile will be a carriage without horses nor mules. It will have a fiery engine of great power to propel it faster than any horse can. You will sit inside out of the weather as comfortable as at home by the fire and it will come in any color you want."

"Any color!"

They all believed him. It must have been his dignified appearance. Maybe it was his lined face and straight back. No one in that township could talk as well as he.

"Water will be so cheap you will hose down your driveway with it."

"But that would make ruts in my driveway and I don't want ruts."

"In two hundred years hence your driveway will be paved with artificial rock. It will be flat, hard and as smooth as you want. The dirt will wash off, the artificial stone driveway will remain.

"Your wife will not have to use the scrub board for hours every week - she will have a machine to wash the clothes. She will have a stove for cooking that will require neither wood nor coal - turn a dial and one of four burners on the top gets hot enough to cook beef stew with carrots and potatoes. There will be an oven where your wife will be able to pick the temperature she wants and go on to something else without checking the firebox.

"You won't have to chop wood anymore as warm air will flow to every room of your house.

"Average people will be so rich they will be able to buy their food in stores, sometimes already prepared or partially prepared.

"At night you can put your oil lamps and candles away because you will touch a switch on the wall and instantly the room will be filled with the light of a hundred candles. Your wife will be able to sew her most delicate sewing, and both of you will be able to read as though it was daylight."

"I could read my Bible at night after work!"

"New medicines will cure smallpox, diphtheria and a hundred other plagues of today. People will live longer, more than seventy years on the average."

"Wow, seventy years on the average!"

"Farmers will have great carriages driven by fiery engines that will pull large plows faster than any mule can. One farmer with the fiery engine will be able to do the work of ten men producing such an abundance of food that the price will go down. Most people will work in easier jobs in factories, offices and stores. The average work week will be just forty-four hours, leaving many hours for leisure activities.

"The abundance of food will replace the age old problem of famine and starvation with the problem of obesity as people will eat too much food, especially beef, pork, milk, cake, candy and water in bottles with sugar and flavoring."

"With water coming out of pipes in your home good for drinking, why would people drink water in bottles with sugar and flavoring?"

"Mainly it will be because plain water will be so cheap it will be perceived as not as good as water in bottles that you have to pay extra for.

"You will be able to travel to Richmond and back in one day in your automobile with your family."

They all marvelled at these tales. Ezra said, "We shall all be happy then. No one will complain ever again."

"No, Mr. Proprietor. Two hundred years hence in the year 1992 people will not be as happy as today."

"Impossible," said John.

"That couldn't be," said Clyde.

The old man continued, "They will complain that they cannot buy enough things. They will complain that the things they do buy cost too much and that they don't make them as well as formerly. With the new and marvelous medicines even their dogs will receive better medical care than King George gets today, yet they will complain about their medical care."

"I haven't seen a doctor in five years," said Caleb.

"I haven't seen a doctor in all my life," said Warren.

"Great organizations who speak to you through the sound boxes and the moving picture boxes in your homes and who write in your newspapers will point out how dire the situation is and how each month a new crisis presents itself that can only be solved if politicians are allowed to take control."

"Now, old man," said John, "I believed everything you said up until now for I have a brain God gave me to use. I know if people had the abundance you described they would not complain but would be happy and content and would thank God every hour for their good fortune."

Warren's tone showed a little anger, "Look stranger, you're beginning to get on my nerves. At first I thought you were entertaining but I see now by your manner that you expect us to believe that hogwash you're telling. I don't like it none at all. If what you said at first was true then what you said at last was false because everyone here would be happy and content if they had one half of what you said people will have in 1992."

Even the affable Caleb's tone was a little caustic as he said, "It just don't make sense that any great organization that speaks through the sound box, the picture box and the newspapers would fail to thank God for all the wonderful things you describe that we don't have today."

"Well now," said Ezra, "You presented yourself so well you had me believing you all along you. But now I see you're not telling the truth because every man here knows that when he has all those wondrous things you say he will have and also even has extra time after he finishes his work then we all know he will be happy and not complain. Why would people need politicians to solve their problems when, the way you say it, people will not have one-tenth the problems they have now?

"You keep what we gave you because we're not a people to go back on our word. And I'll make you corn cakes and give you jerky in the morning. And you can sleep on the floor here tonight.

"But in the morning I expect you to leave and not come back with your grand tales and false prophecies."

MARGI'S PROBLEM

She had met Steve and liked him a lot. He was coming over tonight. He wanted to meet her father. But she and her mother were the entire household. Margi had an idea.

She walked across the street to her friend Rachael's house. Inside Rachael, lounging in a chair and watching Oprah, heard a knocking, "Who's there?"

"It's me, Margi."

"Oh, hi, Margi. Come in. What's up?"

"Rachael, I need your help. Steve wants to meet my father."

"Your father! You never met your father. You don't even know who he is."

"I know that. What I want to ask you is - could I borrow Tom and tell Steve that Tom is my father?"

"Huh, what? Well, why not. When?"

"Steve is coming at seven tonight."

Carl Charbonnet

"I'll have Tom there at six, forty-five."
"Thanks, Rachael."

~~~~~~~~~~~~~~~~~~~~~~~~~~~

As they waited the only sound was Margi's mother's rocking chair creaking on the floor. Tom sat silently, hands clutching chair arms, eyes straight ahead. Margi fidgeted in her chair as she looked at Tom.

"Tom, shouldn't you be reading a newspaper or something," asked Margi.

"Hey, I don't read."

"Maybe if you were smoking a pipe?"

"Are you nuts? Who smokes pipes?"

"Well, what do fathers do?"

"The ones I know leave town. Hey, what're you fidgeting about?"

"This doesn't look right. I'm five-seven, and you're five-six. Shouldn't a father be taller than his daughter?"

"Just tell him I'm your short father."

"And you have blue eyes. Mine are brown."

"My hair is dark brown and yours is blond. It averages out."

"Maybe so, but not the height."

"Well. It's too late now," said Margi's mother. "I heard a car door slam."

"And," said Tom, "Somebody's coming up the walkway to the front door."

Margi's Problem

Margi nervously went to the door and opened it, "Steve, come in."

"Hi Margi. You look nice tonight. But you're all tensed up, is something wrong?"

"Oh no, nothing's wrong. It's just that I never introduced my father to anyone before. Steve, this is my father."

"Hi, Mr. Wainright," said Steve as he reached out his hand. "It sure is good to meet Margi's father."

"Yeah, well ..."

"You already know my mother, Steve."

"Of course. How are you tonight, Mrs. Wainright?"

"Just fine, Steve."

"Haven't I met you somewhere before, Mr. Wainright?"

"I hope not. Where could we have possibly met?"

"At the poolroom."

"I never go to no poolroom."

"What kind of work do you do, Mr. Wainright?"

"Hey, look, I'm the father. Let me ask the questions."

"Of course. I'm sorry."

"What do you do, young man?"

"I work at Bruno's in produce. It's a good job. I like it."

Margi blurted out, "My father is a carpenter."

"Good, that's good, that's real good," said Steve.

Tom stood up, "Time for me to go now." He walked towards Margi with both hands forward, "Marge, kiss your dad good night."

Carl Charbonnet

"Huh?

Mrs. Wainright jumped up and quickly forced her-self between them, "Honey Bun, daughters don't do that anymore. Don't you remember?"

"Don't leave because of me, Mr. Wainright."

"Got to go to work."

"Work. A carpenter who works at night?" wondered Steve aloud.

"Yeah, it's a rush job over on Tenth Avenue."

"Near the poolroom?"

"I told you I don't play no pool. Are you trying to be smart with me. If you are, I might not let Margi go out with you anymore."

"T..., Dad. Please," said Margi.

"No, sir. I was just trying to think which new house is under construction on Tenth Avenue."

"It ain't no new house. We're adding a room inside an old house. That's why we can work at night, don't you see."

"It's perfectly clear. Well, good night Mr. Wainright."

"Good night to you, and don't keep, uh . . . my daughter out too late."

"No, Sir," Steve said, as Tom left.

"How about some cheese sandwiches," asked Mrs. Wainright.

"Oh, not cheese again," said Margi.

"But cheese don't cost nothing, not even stamps. They give you all you want since three weeks ago. I

Margi's Problem

thought of selling some but everybody already had theirs."

"We're going to go out, Mrs. Wainright. Thank you anyway."

"I'll get my coat."

Steve helped Margi on with her coat and said as they left, "Good night Mrs. Wainright."

"Good night, Steve. Come back any time."

"How long," said Steve after the Honda started, "has your father been a carpenter?"

"Why all these questions about my father? Don't you have any questions about me?"

"I'm just interested in your family, that's all. What did your grandfather do?"

"Grandfather!"

"Yeah, your grandfather. What did he do?"

"Why, he was a carpenter too. And so was his father. And so was his father's father. They were all carpenters. Now that should stop those kind of questions."

"What kind of questions?"

"Questions about my father and my grandfather, that kind of question."

Steve turned left on Tenth Avenue. The poolroom was ahead on the right. A man was entering, "Hey, isn't that your father going into the poolroom?"

"No, that's T . . , no, that's not my father. My father's taller than him."

"I thought your father was short."

Carl Charbonnet

"Are you calling my father short?"

"Margi, I'm just talking. I saw a guy going into the pool room who was the same size as your father and wearing the same color shirt, and you get angry."

"I'm not angry. It's just that all you want to do is talk about my father."

"Well, here we are," he said as he turned right into the parking lot of Louie's, Open All Nite, Beer, Dancing and Sandwiches. As they got out of the car they could hear the music coming from inside.

Inside young people talked and laughed, and three couples danced on the small dance floor. Tables were crowded close together around the dance floor. They found an empty table and sat down. A friend at the adjoining table said, "Hey Margi. I saw Tom go in your house at six-thirty. Is he dating your mother now?"

"Charlene," answered Margi, "What a nice blue dress. Is it new?"

"Hey, why don't you two sit at our table?"

Steve stood up, "Thanks." They moved to Charlene's table.

"This is Bobby," said Charlene, "Bobby - Margi. I don't know the good looking one."

"This is Steve."

"Where you been hiding him?"

"I haven't been hiding him."

"Was that guy I saw enter your house dating your mother?'

Margi's Problem

"Tonight everybody wants to talk about my parents. This is not parent talking about night. This is having fun night. Let's have fun. Dance with me, Steve."

"We haven't ordered yet."

Margi moved her chair close to Steve, so close her thigh touched his along its entire length. She put her mouth to his ear and whispered, "I want to dance with you and get close to you with my body so everybody can see us dancing close."

That did it. He stood up. They walked the four feet to the dance floor. Margi stayed a few inches away as they danced.

"What happened to the passion?"

"I just wanted to get away from that table, that's all."

"Do you want to move to another table and sit alone together?"

"No. I want to sit with them, have fun and not talk about my parents. Let's sit down and order."

The waitress came over.

"What do you want, Margi?" asked Steve.

"What are you having?"

"A Silver Bullet."

"I'll have a Silver Bullet."

"Steve," said Charlene, "If Margi drops you, you can come and see me."

"Charlene!" exclaimed Margi.

"Ten o'clock tomorrow morning is a good time."

"I'll be at work then."

"Work. You work! What do you work for?"

"Huh? Nobody ever asked me that before. I don't know. Everybody works. I guess I work for money for one thing."

"You're a sap. Nobody on my street works. My mother tried it once, and she made less money than staying home."

"How do you make money staying home then working?"

"And they say blonds are dumb," said Charlene. "How about cute guys who don't know anything? We have here a real male bimbo.

"Look Steve, I'll try to explain it. You go register. Well, I guess it's easier for a woman. They ask a woman if she has any children. You say yes. They ask her if she has a husband. You say no. They ask her if she has a job. You say no. They say, 'Sign this.' From then on you get checks in the mail, all as regular as day and night. It adds up to more money than working."

"Do you and Bobby have children?"

"Not us, me. I have a little boy."

"Bobby's not the father?"

"Of course not. If he was I wouldn't say."

"Hmm. What do you do, Bobby?"

"I hang around."

"You don't have a job?"

"No man."

"Why not?"

Margi's Problem

"I'd rather hang around and drink beer."

"You mean Charlene gets checks in the mail and is supporting you and you loaf?"

"Let's say, I'm a man of leisure. Look, you'd do the same if you could. Maybe you could move in with Margi."

"But we're not married."

"Ha, ha, ha, ha," laughed Charlene and Bobby.

"Margi's father works," said Steve "He's a carpenter."

"Man, where you been," said Bobby, "Margi don't even know . . . "

Margi abruptly got up, pulled Steve's arm as she said, "I want to dance real close." After the dance she said, "I don't want to sit with them anymore. I want to sit with you, alone over in that dark corner."

They spent the rest of the time by themselves.

~~~~~~~~~~~~~~~~~~~~~~~~~~

It was dark in front of Margi's house and dark inside too. Margi's pulse quickened with anticipation as they walked from the car to the porch.

"Good night, Margi."

"You're coming in, aren't you."

"Not tonight."

The young, good-looking Margi moved towards Steve with passion and verve.

Steve backed up and said, "Margi, I want my life to

amount to something."

"You mean," she said sarcastically, "you're going to work hard and become president of the company and be rich?"

"I'm going to work hard, but I don't think it's in the cards for me to become rich. That's not the main thing.

"The main thing is that I'll be a worker earning my own living. Someday I'll have a wife. We'll have a couple of kids and a three-bedroom, one-bath house with red roses in front. Each evening, at the dinner table, I'll lead the family in prayer."

"You're crazy," said Margi.

"Maybe so," said Steve as he walked to his car, "But I have to get up early tomorrow and go to work."

THE GOOD ABORTIONIST

He saved the lives of nine babies.

One Morning he woke up sick with a virus and didn't go to work.

MORALITY CANNOT BE LEGISLATED

Morality cannot be legislated. Everybody knows that.

No one has the right to impose his or her unique morality on the rest of us.

But did you know that in the dark ages before the 1960's, people held the myth that morality could be legislated?

I'm Frank Remington, the holder of more Ph.D.s than anyone in history, all from top schools. I have Ph.D.s in Psychology, Sociology, Political Science, English Literature (specializing in left-handed writers) and am the only holder in the entire country of a Ph.D in the History of Progress. So I know what I am talking about and what I am talking about is the history of progress.

Now I'll admit that great scholars have differing opinions on exactly when progress began. Some say

Carl Charbonnet

progress began in 1917 when the workers of Russia rid themselves of the shackles of greedy capitalism and began living in bliss. The date I like to use is 1960. The decade of the sixties is the decade of freedom from the shackles of morality.

Before 1960, the era I call Before Political Correctness or B.P.C., you would not believe the trouble we were in. Children were allowed to bring the Bible to school. Before Political Correctness, teachers were permitted to tack the Ten Commandments on the classroom bulletin board.

I have a confession to make. I used to think I was the smartest person alive with my Ph.D.s and all. But now I take my hat off to the glorious justices of the Supreme Court. They looked at the Constitution and saw "Separation of Church and State." If you get a copy of the Constitution and look it up you won't find it because you're not smart enough. Common people should not be allowed to read the Constitution. The Supreme Court justices are smarter than you or I and they found it, they took action. On June 17, 1963, they censored the Bible and prayer from primary and secondary public schools.[1]

This opened the floodgates of progress as school boards and writers of textbooks proceeded to cleanse our history texts of everything we don't want children to learn – from Paul Revere to the Judeo-Christian influence in the founding of our country. If they had-

Morality Cannot Be Legislated

n't cleansed the history books of the overwhelming part Judeo-Christianity played in our society, think of the trouble we would be in today.

A seven year old girl was arrested in Indiana for reading her Bible on the school bus. Nip them in the bud, get rid of them root and branch, I say. That's what the government is for.

President Lyndon Johnson was such a fine man - so truthful, so caring, so progressive - that he started the War on Poverty. Over five trillion dollars have been compassionately spent to raise the poor above the poverty line. There are those who say that because there are more poor people today than before the government began helping them, the program has been a failure. Those people just don't get it. Those same uncaring, old-fashioned greedy types, who want to raise the taxes of the poor and lower the taxes of the rich, claim that it was because the government took over the father's role in many families that there has been a decline in the family structure and a concomitant increase in crime. Nothing could be further from the truth. I have more Ph.D.s than any one in the world and I say that the more the government destroys the family structure, the lower the crime rate. Is that clear enough?

And we must applaud and cherish the American Civil Liberties Union for seeking out and destroying representations of the Christ Child on courthouse

Carl Charbonnet

lawns each Christmas Season. How thoughtful its members are.

Congratulations also to those wonderful sex educators who, always caring about our children, give them condoms to protect them from inconvenient diseases.

Planned Parenthood deserves credit, too, because it has gone to court to stop schools from teaching chastity. Everyone should write their congressman or congresswoman to urge them to continue sending millions of tax dollars to Planned Parenthood.

For over a century a small group of religious fanatics had been imposing its morality on the rest of us by seeing to it that States had various laws interfering with a woman's right to have an abortion. But in 1973, in its infinite wisdom, the justices of the Supreme Court properly ignored their oaths of offices to uphold the Constitution and negated those State laws when they decreed that no State had the right to interfere with any woman, at any time, if she wanted to kill her baby while it resided within her body. Abortion upon demand from conception through nine months to the day before birth became legal. Today over a million babies a year are being generously saved from the horror of living. Progress has been made - and Planned Parenthood deserves additional credit for operating so many abortuaries. That's another reason to write your congressman or congresswoman: request that more millions be sent to

Morality Cannot Be Legislated

Planned Parenthood so it can open even more abortuaries and save even more babies from the horror of living.

We must be vigilant. In 1995 the ultra right Christian Coalition lobbied against partial birth abortions. That's a late term abortion where the doctor pulls out the legs and torso of the fetus so that he can get at the head while the head is still inside. He pushes a scissors into the head at the base of the skull and opens it. Then he inserts a vacuum thing into the opening and sucks out the brain.

Partial birth abortions are perfectly legal, yet the Christian Coalition objects to them. What's the matter with those people?

In reaction to such extremists, in 1999, the Care America Party was formed and dedicated to the principle that every vestige of morality and, or, religion that remained in our laws must be rooted out.

The New York Courier-Ledger announced, "NEW PARTY CARES, IT'S ABOUT TIME." The newspaper editors endorsed the Care America Party and the dominant media followed their lead.

The first year the Care America Party offered candidates, five representatives were sent to Washington. Two years later that number was thirty-four, with six Care America Party candidates going to the Senate. That was not enough to break gridlock; a majority was needed and it soon appeared.

Carl Charbonnet

When Care America Party's candidate, Frank Covington was elected President, he went to Washington with a majority in both houses. The Care America Party had a mandate. It lost no time searching this country's laws for vestiges of legislated morality.

President Covington was brilliant. He had a probing mind that missed nothing. So when he happened to come upon a dusty copy of the Ten Commandments and noticed Commandment VIII - Thou shalt not steal – the words jumped off the page into his mind. His passion erupted as he thought, *How could this have gone on unnoticed for so long? All fifty States have been forcing Judeo-Christian morality on the rest of us.*

As I said President Covington was brilliant. He reasoned that if he went to the Congress, with his proposal to negate the laws of fifty States on stealing, some right-wing, Christian extremists might cause gridlock and prevent passage. He knew a quicker way to legislation. He planned a star studded lunch and invited the five Supreme Court justices he knew would not fulfill their oaths of office to uphold the Constitution.

~~~~~~~~~~~~~~~~~~~~~~~~~

When the limousines drove up to the White House portico delivering the Justices President Covington became agitated.. "I don't hear music," he said to the head of the Secret Service, "where is my favorite band, Dead Slop and Proud Of It?"

"I'll find out, Sir," the Secret Service chief said as he sharply left.

In ninety seconds he returned. "Sir, I solved the problem. A new agent, fresh from Montana, was manning the door when Dead Slop and Proud Of It arrived. He thought they were either deranged street people or Iranian terrorists and arrested them. He's been holding them in a broom closet but they've been released on my order and are now setting up to play.

"Thanks, Al," said the President and in a few minutes the band's music could be heard by the arriving guests.

In the dining room the justices mingled with Hollywood luminaries. Famous journalists fawned over the five guests of honor from the land's highest court. Joe Sumerstone, himself, put his arm around Justice's Fred Leftward's shoulder and complimented him on how much he had matured since coming to Washington. He thanked the justice for his enlightened vote that protected the First Amendment rights of pornography and his other enlightened vote to censor the Bible from schools.

After an hour of drinking and an hour of eating, famous Hollywood comedian Pristine entertained the group with really funny jokes about mayhem, excrement and this one - "What's the difference between a

Carl Charbonnet

Christian Minister and an orangutan? The orangutan isn't trying to tell you how to live your life HAR, HAR, HAR."

The guests quieted and got serious as President Covington rose and began speaking. "We have removed the Ten Commandments from the school-room bulletin board. But our work is not finished," he noted. Since I care for you and feel your pain I am always studying ways to help you and bring the good life to America. In the course of my studies I have learned something shocking - I have discovered that the VIIIth Commandment says, 'Thou shalt not steal.'"

"Oohh, aaww!"

"Now, keep calm, everybody. Don't panic. I know what you're thinking - that we can't have religious fanatics forcing their morality on us. But today, 1998, all fifty Sates have laws against stealing. I am asking the five Supreme Court Justices present here now to again forget their oaths of office, to uphold the Constitution; and do their duty and nullify all the States laws related to stealing."

President Covington got a standing ovation.

~~~~~~~~~~~~~~~~~~~~~~~~~~

A Cleveland man named Leatherwood stood before the picture window in his living room holding a news-paper in his left hand as he scratched his head with his

Morality Cannot Be Legislated

right. He looked out of the window, and saw someone hot-wiring his car. He heard the engine start. He flung the newspaper to the floor and ran outside.

The man was attempting to drive away, but he was between another car and a tree, going back and forth to get out of the tight parking space. Leatherwood reached the car, opened the door and dragged out the thief. He held him on the ground as his wife called the police.

A police car arrived and two officers got out, "What's going on here?" one asked.

"That man my husband is holding on the ground was caught red handed stealing our car," said Mrs. Leatherwood.

The officer looked down at both of the men as he scratched his chin. Then he bent down and tapped Mr. Leatherwood on the shoulder and said to him, "You have the right to remain silent. If you say anything it might be used against you. You have the right to an attorney."

Turning to the other officer he said, "Give me a hand here, Bob." Together they lifted Mr. Leatherwood off the thief.

As the police were putting the cuffs on Mr. Leatherwood he protested, "Wait, I'm the victim, my wife called you! That man is the one you should arrest, he was stealing my car."

"Don't you know," said the officer, "The Supreme Court has ruled that everybody has the right to steal.

Carl Charbonnet

It's an individual's choice. All laws restricting a person's right to steal are invalid.

Then he turned to Mrs. Leatherwood, "Mrs. Leatherwood, since you conspired to prevent this fine man from exercising his right of freedom of choice to steal, we will have to take you in also." The offices put handcuffs on Mrs. Leatherwood too, and led the couple to the police car.

"Wait!" shouted the thief. "I need the keys so I won't have to keep hot-wiring this car."

"Well," said one of the officers, "What do you want me to do?"

"Hold him while I take the keys from his pocket," replied the thief.

"Can't see anything wrong with that, can you, Fred?"

"Seems perfectly legal to me, Bob."

So they held Mr. Leatherwood while the thief went through his pockets until he found the keys, "Thanks, fellows, you're sure fine officers. Have a nice day." He walked to the car, got in and drove away.

The three Leatherwood children, Ellen, Sandy and Mark, with their hands on the window sill and their faces to the glass, watched as their handcuffed parents were loaded into the back of the police car and driven away.

[1] Since reversed by the petition of Jay Sekulow of The American Center for Law And Justice founded by Pat Robertson.

ARMS

Ivan was an active boy of twelve who enjoyed walking in the woods that surrounded his village. It was 1950 in the Soviet Union and warm for January. At noon the temperature went just above freezing. He put on his coat and went out in the snow.

The railroad tracks passed just a hundred meters from his house. Often he walked along the tracks because it was easier. This time, since he had more than two hours before dark, he decided he would head straight into the woods, turn south and intersect the tracks. That way, if it got dark before he reached home, he would have no trouble following the rails back to his village.

Deep into the woods he went. He never understood why, but something inside him soaked up the ambiance of the forest and made him feel good.

As he continued up a gentle but long incline, he

Carl Charbonnet

became so warm he opened the front of his coat to let the air in. He even took off his coat for a time, carrying it slung over his shoulder.

He walked farther into the woods than he had ever walked before. He saw different trees and bushes. After some time in the unfamiliar woods, he turned south and headed for the tracks.

The land became flatter as he continued, and the sun went lower in the sky. He became anxious lest it get dark before he reached the tracks.

His spirits elevated when ahead he saw the clearing for the tracks. After a short distance, the tracks themselves appeared, He stepped between the rails on the ties and headed west toward his village.

After a short distance he was surprised to see a boxcar standing alone on a siding. *I didn't know there was a siding out here,* he thought. *I wonder why? there's no town here.* As he approached the car he saw it was old and damaged, with several cracks in the wooden sides. Things could be seen sticking out through some of the cracks.

The low lying sun was no longer bright. The details of the boxcar were indistinct. He walked closer. *What's in the car,* he wondered, *firewood?* He was determined to find out.

The first thing he examined appeared to be an arm-sized branch with a crook. *It looks like an elbow of a person!* He moved along the side of the car when in

Arms

front of him something with fingers stuck out farther than the others.

It's a hand!

The twelve year old fell back feeling faint. When he got control of himself he walked closer. He returned to the first thing he had seen, moved closer until his eyes were a few centimeters away. He saw, for sure, that it was an arm. He moved parallel to the side of the car and saw arm after arm. *It's a boxcar full of arms!*

As the realization of what he had seen reached his innermost parts, he backed off again. He turned, dropped to the ground on his hands and knees and vomited into the snow.

He wanted to run but curiosity held him. He looked on the ground for a stick. He found a stiff one. With this strong stick he approached the car and poked at one of the arms. It was frozen solid from the previous night's cold. He walked up and down. He could see that the car was full from top to bottom with arms, nothing but arms.

He had seen enough. He headed for home.

~~~~~~~~~~~~~~~~~~~~~~~~~~~

At the dinner table he stuck his spoon into the porridge, lifted it and put it back again without eating. His mother noticed, "What's the matter, Ivan, are you sick?"

Carl Charbonnet

"I saw a boxcar full of arms."

"Huh?" his father questioned.

"I saw a boxcar full of arms."

"A boxcar full of arms! You mean a train passed and one of the cars was a boxcar that was full of something that looked like arms?"

"No. The boxcar was on a siding. It was farther into the woods than where I usually walk."

"But there is no siding out in the woods as far as I know. Are you saying there's a town a few kilometers east that I don't know about?"

"There was no town. Just a boxcar on a siding."

His father put down his spoon and spoke carefully. "Ivan, what you say is very unusual. I have never heard of a siding a few kilometers east of here, and if there is a siding I cannot imagine why there would be a boxcar full of arms."

"I know, Father. I got sick and vomited. I don't feel well now."

"Son, next week on my day off, I'll go with you so you can show me what you saw."

"I will, Father. But in a week it might be gone."
"In the meantime I don't want you to mention this to anyone else, not even to your friend Denesovich."

~~~~~~~~~~~~~~~~~~~~~~~~~~

The temperature was well below freezing, so Ivan and his father left in midmorning so it would still be

Arms

light and relatively warm by the time their trip was completed. They walked along the tracks on the way out so they wouldn't miss the siding in the woods.

The trees were thick on both sides of the tracks as they briskly walked. When they heard a train coming from around the bend Ivan's father said, "Ivan, quick," and they both ran into the woods and hid.

The click-ed-de-clack of the train got louder and then roared as it came along side of them. The sound diminished becoming fainter and fainter as the train disappeared from sight. "If someone on the train had seen us, he might have wondered what we were doing way out here and reported us. Then men would come looking for us and ask questions. Are we getting close to the siding, Ivan?"

"Maybe two more kilometers."

After a half hour Ivan's father said, "There it is." He was relieved at the sight of it now knowing that his son really had seen a siding with a box car on it. But he still was not prepared for what he was to examine.

Quickly he walked to the boxcar and up and down along both sides of it. He put his face up to a crack and looked in as far as he could see, which wasn't far at all because the car was packed. It was just as Ivan had described it. "There must be thousands of arms here. But why?"

"I don't know. Father."

He took his son aside and spoke gravely, "Ivan, lis-

Carl Charbonnet

ten to me. This is very important, "Do you remember Pugachev?"

"Yes, Father."

"Do you remember Ramzin?"

"Yes, I do."

"Ramzin saw the men come and take away Pugachev. Then he told a few people about it. A week later they took Ramzin away too. We have not heard from either of them since that time.

"So we will both forget what we have seen, what we know to be the truth. When we get home I will tell your mother, and then the three of us will never mention it again. Do you understand?"

"Yes, father."

DIOGENES LOOKING FOR
AN EDUCATED MAN

DIOGENES

Diogenes awoke. He was sitting on the ground with his back against a tree. He rubbed his eyes and looked around.

At first everything was fuzzy, out of focus. Then he became aware of a group of people nearby. He heard them talking. They were talking about him. "He wasn't here yesterday," said one.

"I passed here forty minutes ago and he wasn't here then,." said another.

"Look," said a third, "he's waking up." They remained silent as Diogenes looked around.

Well, I'm amidst a group of grown children strangely dressed, he thought as he sat upright. "Hello, children," he said.

"Hello old man. Where did you get those duds?"

"Duds?"

"That dress you're wearing."

"Oh, my chiton. Yes, I know. It is not as fine as the ones the merchants wear. I bought it two years ago at the market near the Acropolis from a man named Artantes who overcharged me."

"But why are you dressed that way?"

"I am astonished at your question because all of you are dressed in a most peculiar way that I have never before seen, even at the theatre. Would you explain why you are dressed as you are?"

They chuckled at the old man's incomprehensible answer. Then one said, "We're dressed this way because this is the way we dress, the way everybody dresses."

Diogenes looked around. There were other people passing along smooth, stone walkways, dressed in a manner similar to these children. He turned his head in the direction of a loud, ominous noise that was getting louder as it got closer. His eyes focused upon a strange, smoking chariot with a man riding it but without horses. As he stared in disbelief he noticed that as the chariot moved it cut a swath in the grass short and astonishingly even. "What a marvelous chariot," he exclaimed. "What do you call it?"

More chuckling, "Why, it's a lawn mower."

"A lawn mower?"

"Yes, it cuts grass, don't you see?"

"I do see. It is marvelous, but I am confused."

The laughter was louder than before.

These children think I am confused, and so I am. I

am bewildered. *I feel as though I have awoken from a long sleep and am none the worse for it but have found myself in some strange land of which I have never been nor ever heard.* "What year is this?"

"It's 1994."

"Nineteen ninety-four. I don't understand."

The lawn mower and its noise had stopped. The man riding it spoke, "1994 A.D., the year of our Lord. The way you are dressed is typical of the way the ancient Greeks dressed."

At last hearing something that made sense, Diogenes rose. "Yes, I am Greek and though old I think ancient is a bit too much."

"Sir, I meant no offense. By ancient Greece I mean the civilization that existed about 2,400 years ago or so. Looking at you sir," said the gardener, "the way you are dressed and seeing the lantern on the ground beside you lit, though the sun shines brightly, brings to mind Diogenes."

"Oh, sir," he said as he walked to the gardener with outstretched arms, "Thank you, I *am* Diogenes. Tell me, where am I?"

"You are at Bovundy University."

"University? What is a university?"

"A university is a place where people come to get educated."

"And do they get it, Sir?"

"Why, you even talk like Diogenes would. I'm

Carl Charbonnet

sixty-four now and when I went to the university I think some of us got an education. It is different today and I'm not sure."

"Different how?"

"Well, for one thing basic courses of Western Civilization are not stressed anymore. Some students never learn at all about ancient Greece." Then turning to the students, "Have any of you heard of Diogenes?"

No one answered. Then he asked, "Aristotle?"

"I've heard of him," said one.

"And what have you heard?"

"Well, I can't think of anything really. We study multiculturalism."

"What's multiculturalism?" asked Diogenes.

"Well, let's see," pondered the student. "When you have completed a course in multiculturalism you realize how rotten your own country is and has been and how wonderful other societies, different from ours, are."

Diogenes, seldom at a loss for words, was stunned. He changed the subject, "I know Aristotle. He's the wisest man in Athens."

"What's Athens?" asked one of the students.

"Athens is the capital of Greece," said the gardener. "In the fifth century B.C. the City State of Athens developed the greatest civilization the world to that time had known. Athenians excelled in science, politics, philosophy and art. You might say they invented modern scientific inquiry. As for politics, they invented democracy. In philosophy they made systematic inquiry into the nature of man and society. As for art, I have seen samples of what this university calls art, and can say that the art of Athens of 2,400 years ago is superior to the art of Bovundy University of today."

"If you're so smart why are you cutting grass and not teaching?"

"Children," broke in Diogenes, "have respect for your elders."

"Old man, you have been insulting us by calling us children since you awoke."

"I'm sorry if that offended you. What do you prefer I call you?"

"Students will do."

"Students, you have not heard of Diogenes? Have you heard of Pericles?"

The gardener nodded as one student answered, "No."

"And you sir. Can you tell the students what I am famous for."

"The one thing that I am aware of that I would say you are famous for is for going to the marketplace in the daytime with a lighted lantern looking for an honest man."

Diogenes was beginning to accept the idea that he was in a different age, one removed by time from his own. "Is that the one thing you recall? Yes, I did say that one day to make a point. It caused quite a stir."

The students were beginning to leave without a word until one turned and said, "Sir, it was good to talk with you. I must go to class now."

"Thank you, young student." Then questioning the gardener, "The boys were students but what were the girls doing here?"

"They are students too."

"Strange, this nineteen ninety-four of yours. And Sir, you seem educated. Why are you not a teacher instead of a grass cutter as one of them rudely pointed out?"

"There is no mystery about it. I am an alcoholic."

"I don't know what that is."

"I am addicted to alcohol."

"Oh, yes. I have known others who have thus fallen. You seem sober now."

"I am trying. I have not had a drink in three years, the longest since my fall. Before my fall I was an accountant, had a family, a fine house and a good life, which I failed to appreciate until I lost it."

"Are you optimistic about your future or pessimistic?"

"Optimistic."

"To what do you credit the change?"

"Most of my life I was without direction, without principles and self-centered. Now I am devoted to God and try to love my neighbor as myself."

"Which God - Apollo, Athena, Zeus?"

Diogenes

"In America today, those of us who believe, believe there is only one God."

"How quaint, one God only. Hardly seems adequate. What is your one God's name?"

"It is a little complicated. Even before your time the Hebrews determined there was one God, a moral God. Those of my faith, Christianity, which is rooted in the Hebrew faith, call him God, we call him Jesus, yet they are father and son."

"Sir, you appear to be doing well now, and I truly wish that you have permanently resisted the temptation and that soon you will find a job more suitable to your intellect.

"Let me say that the students I have just met seem very ignorant compared to students in Athens. There they thirsted for knowledge and understanding and did, in some cases, acquire it. These students seem so vacuous. But I presume their teachers are educated. With the academy's gardener as decent and informed as you, I expect all the teachers to be the superiors of Aristotle."

"Well," the gardener said, "not necessarily."

"Is this the only academy in this strange land?"

"No, there are hundreds."

"And is this one that you call Bovundy University one of the better or one of the worse?"

"The consensus says it is *the* best."

"Good. Then I know what I must do.

"You have indicated that the teachers are not as

well educated as the fine buildings indicate. So I shall
take my lighted lantern and visit this academy to see
how quickly I can locate an educated man." Diogenes
began walking away, then turned, to address the gardener and two passing students, "Pass the word,
Diogenes is looking for an educated man at the consensus best university in this land."

Diogenes walked along the cement path to a large
building. *Not so impressive as the Parthenon but
impressive in its own way. It looks sturdy with good
proportion. The covering by vines gives it a comfortable appearance.* He walked up a wide stairway and
entered.

Near the entrance was an opened door to an office.
He went in.

A young woman at a desk looked up. Astonished
but respectful, she smiled, "May I help you?"

"Yes, young lady. I am Diogenes. Would you tell
me who is the wisest teacher here?"

"Humm," she cleared her throat. "Let's see, Dr.
Markstead is department head. Perhaps he is the one
you have in mind."

"May I see Dr. Markstead?"

"I'll ring him."

Ring him? Ring him? What could she mean?

"Dr. Markstead, there is a man wearing a baggy
dress who would like to speak with you. He says his
name is Diogenes."

Dr. Markstead in his office was taken back. *Oh no,*

*another campus demonstrator. Well, I don't want to
get in any trouble with those people.* "Send him in,
Ms. Doster."

Dr. Markstead was prepared when he arrived,
"Come in. Diogenes, you said, did you not?"

"Yes, I have arrived in your strange land just today
and am still bewildered by all the new things I have
seen."

"Take a seat, Mr. Diogenes. But before we talk let
me point out that the university is low on funds this
year. The Government has not been progressive."

"Forgive me, doctor, but I have not learned your
dialect yet. What are 'funds'?"

"The budget, money, we are very restricted in our
disbursements."

"How has the Government not been progressive?"

"They have not given us enough money, of course.
This year the increase was only three percent."

"Oh, no matter. My visit is of other things."

"What is the purpose of your visit then, Mr.
Diogenes?"

"To ask you a few questions, if I may."

"Why, of course."

"Dr. Markstead, what is the purpose of your university?"

"Humph. Why . . . the purpose, of my university?"
What a strange question. This fellow is up to something.
"The purpose of Bovundy, as of all universities, is to

Carl Charbonnet

teach the students that we must work for the good of the world, of the entire world and of the environment. We must realize that every tree, every mouse, every blade of grass has rights. We must point out the massive faults of our corrupt society. Our graduates know that a society based on greed must be changed. We must prohibit the students from saying anything that is offensive to any official minority."

"What do you mean by 'official' minority?"

"A minority designated by the elite."

"Can you give an example of such a minority?"

"Blacks and women."

"Women. I would have thought women outnumbered men. I'm surprised to learn that men now outnumber women."

"Men don't outnumber women. There are more women than men."

"But I thought you said women were a minority?"

"Believe me, Mr. Diogenes, women are a minority. It's hard to explain it to someone dressed in an old sheet like you are."

"May I continue. Can you tell me, if you wish, what is the purpose of government?"

"Why to direct and control society and solve all its problems, of course."

"And how about the marketplace?"

"The marketplace must be controlled. That is the purpose of government. Business needs governmental direction. The country needs a plan. All of our students know that business without government control is chaotic, greedy and exploitative."

"Dr. Markstead. it would help me if I had a list of the other teachers. Would it be impertinent of me to request of you such a list?"

Relieved that the interview seemed to be nearing the end without a crisis, Dr. Markstead gladly complied.

~~~~~~~~~~~~~~~~~~~~~~~~~~~

Each time Diogenes sought a professor he marveled that the one he sought was available. As he took a seat in Professor Dalton's office he asked, "I am surprised that you and the other professors are not in class, are not now teaching students."

"My six graduate students do the teaching. I study and write papers. That is a full load. I don't have time to waste on undergraduates."

"And what do you study?"

"I am a scholar of English Literature. My specialty is the penmanship of Wistercot."

"I have not heard of Mr. Wistercot."

"Well, few people outside of university English departments have heard of him. But let me tell you, no one else utilized the flourish at the end of a word with such beauty, and he dotted his 'i's' with precision."

"Did Mr. Wistercot use his penmanship to say something?"

"That is not in my specialty. Now, don't you think

this has gone far enough? Let me ask you a question.
Why are you wearing a tunic?"

"It's called a chiton. Where I come from that's
what we wear."

"And where do you come from?"

"Athens."

"And where are you going now?"

"I see from the list Dr. Markstead gave me that
Professor Hudson is in the history department. If you
will be so kind as to tell me where Professor Hudson's
office is, I will go there."

"As you go out the door, turn left. Dr. Hudson is in
the next building."

"Thank you," said Diogenes as he left, anticipating
that Dr. Hudson would be more interesting.

~~~~~~~~~~~~~~~~~~~~~~~~~~~

"I am curious," Diogenes said as he got comfortable in Dr. Hudson's office, "What do you teach about
Greece, the Greece of Pericles?"

"Nothing, nothing at all. That is easy to understand
when you realize we teach the history of the glorious
Aztec civilization so cruelly crushed by the
Europeans, as well as the Nigerian epoch, not to mention the pre-European Icelandic civilization. And,
may I remind you," he said with contempt as he
observed Diogenes' lantern, "the Environmental
Protection Agency has twelve regulations against oil-

burning lamps within campus buildings."

Diogenes blew out the lamp, then looked at the professor, "And about your own civilization, what do you call it?"

"We call it Western Civilization. Important studies take so much time that there is little left over for studying Western Civilization."

Astonished he asked, "You don't teach your own civilization?"

"I'm not sure where you are coming from. Did you say you are Mr. Diogenes?"

"Diogenes is my name, and I have come from the Athens of Pericles and Aristotle, though I do not know how."

"May I suggest, Mr. Diogenes, that you visit Dr. Carr. His specialty is Ancient Greek Civilization."

"Thank you sir, I will. That will be exciting. Where is his office?"

"It is in New Age Hall on the other side of the campus. You will want to take the shuttle bus."

"Strange, Dr. Hudson, that you don't study your own civilization, yet you study me so thoroughly that you know I will want to take the shuttle bus. I had not discovered that characteristic myself in myself. I had thought, like Socrates whom my father knew, that I would prefer to walk. That way I can view the university and perhaps meet with more students and teachers on the way."

Carl Charbonnet

Outside the building he relighted his lantern. As he walked he did view the campus. But mostly they viewed him. All eyes watched the man in the tunic with the lighted lantern. He walked and pleasantly greeted each person he passed. Some greeted him, others just stared, a few laughed. Ahead was a group standing, talking. As he approached they stopped talking to look at him. There was an empty bench amid them. "Ah, a bench. May I sit?"

"Nobody else is," said one.

"Of course, please do," said another.

"You have a beautiful university. Never in my life have I seen such grass. It has a neat look about it that is refreshing. I shall tell them about it when I return to Athens."

"It is a lawn like any other. Are you a student here?" one of the students asked Diogenes.

"Yes. I am a student wherever I go."

"Let me put it this way, how long have you been at Bovundy University?"

"Since this morning. I am a visitor. I am Diogenes."

"Are you playing Diogenes in a play?"

"No, this is my way of dressing. This is how we all dress in Athens. Though you are dressed strangely to me, I can tell that you are four boys and five girls." Then looking directly at another student he said, "But as for you, I cannot tell?"

"I am a feminist."

"But these five girls look feminine, and you do not. Why are you called a feminist?"

"I work for women's rights."

"And what are women's rights?"

"Two women marrying and having the same legal status as old-fashioned marriages, having an equal number of women Senators as men, women making the same amount of money as men."

"And how do you think the earnings of men and women should be determined?"

"Why, the courts, of course. That's what courts are for. We need more plaintiff's attorneys and more and larger judgments against men."

"Where I come from, all Senators are men, and women are supported by their husbands. It is the same Sparta, Persia, Egypt and in the other lands."

That brought on laughter.

"You speak as old-fashioned as you dress, old man."

"Thank you," said Diogenes believing he had been complimented.

"And we have to stop the millions of rapes that occur each day," continued the feminist.

Diogenes blushed as he was not accustomed to such talk from a person who had some of the characteristics of a woman. Although he didn't address the problem he did think, *Athens does not have nearly so many rapes as that.*

Carl Charbonnet

He changed the subject by asking the brightest looking boy, "Why are you a student here?"

"Are you kidding? This is the best school in the country. I can take my pick of the top paying jobs when I get my degree."

"And what about education, are you concerned about that?"

"Of course, being here is an education."

"In Athens we believe that education is the achievement of moral character and understanding, not attending school. We believe education is becoming a good man, a moral man, a good citizen. An educated person is one who has learned to love truth, beauty and freedom. You boys and girls are studying to become businessmen?"

"Not I," said one. "I'm going into government service. I can get to be a bureaucrat before I'm twenty-five and at a good salary. By the time I'm thirty-five I expect to supervise hundreds and have a limousine with a phone."

"Why do you want to work in government service, as you put it?"

"Why like I said - because the salary is ample, the pension more than ample, the vacations long and the perks exceptional. The government is big and powerful. Just being a clerk with government gives one a feeling of power. If one is an executive he actually wields power, the higher he goes, the more power.

Diogenes

From there you can look down on the common man."

"But you said you wanted to go into government service; now you talk of power. Would you explain."

"Of course. People need direction, they need government. I would serve them by controlling them."

"And if they don't want to be controlled?"

"They will want to be controlled all right when government pays their housing cost, medical costs, pensions, privileges for labor unions, privileges for businesses, college tuition, subsidies, free lunches and food stamps."

Seldom had anyone's words had such an effect on Diogenes, *And to think I have been called cynical. Never have I felt less proud of it.* He was temporarily at a loss for words as he contemplated what the young man had said.

The student continued, "I want to work for government and - feed the homeless, get rid of poverty, clean up the environment, control greedy businessmen, solve all our problems."

"Has anyone in government ever tried to get rid of poverty before?"

"Well no, because if they had, poverty would have been eliminated."

"Where I come from we attempt to eliminate poverty by working. In Athens and Sparta, as well as Persia and Egypt, women work in the home. May I ask you," he said, addressing one of the girls, "what

Carl Charbonnet

your purpose is here as a student?"

"The same as Bob's, no difference."

"And who will take care of your children?"

"I don't have any, but if I did child care will take care of them." Then, believing she knew how to impress the stranger, she added proudly, "I am going to make a career out of promoting universal public child care."

"And what do you mean by 'public' child care?"

"You know, Washington, D.C. They pay for it and make sure all children get good child care."

"When Plato was a young man he wrote the Republic in which he advocated governmental child care for some of the people. As he matured though age and experience he modified his opinions. Today he might agree with me that wisdom dictates that public child care would destroy the family. Since the family is the most important organization of all, it seems to me you should work as hard as you can against public child care.

"But I must move on. Thank you, students. I am on the way to see Dr. Carr. Is this the way to the New Age Building?"

"Yes, the larger of the three buildings at the end of this path."

"Thank you, boys and girls," he said as he left.

~~~~~~~~~~~~~~~~~~~~~~~~~~~

Diogenes

"Dr. Carr might be a few minutes. Would you like a cup of coffee while you wait?"

"Coffee?"

"Yes, I was drinking coffee when you came in, remember."

"Oh, that would be nice, thank you."

As Diogenes sipped the coffee and waited, he looked around Dr. Carr's office. There were shelves from the floor to the ceiling. Here was a wooden carving, there an Aztec mask, several sets of beads unlike anything he had seen. Nothing was familiar.

The professor was somewhat startled when he saw Diogenes. "My secretary said you were wearing a tunic but said nothing about the lantern. That lantern violates eight regulations from the Environmental Protection Agency. Could you put the thing out."

"If you would like. My point has been made." He blew the lantern out and placed it on the floor.

"Are you in a play or something?"

"No. I am Diogenes. I always dress this way."

"Well, skip it. What do you want?"

"I'm told that your specialty is Ancient Greek Civilization. This flatters me as I think I have somehow come to a civilization many centuries removed from my own. I would like to ask you some questions, and if you would like to ask me some, I might be of help to you."

"How could you possibly be of help to me?"

"I am Greek. I live in Athens. I know Aristotle and

Carl Charbonnet

Plato. My father knew Socrates, Sophocles and Pericles."

"Let me put it this way, what do you want to know from me?"

"What do you teach that is significant about Greek Civilization in the time of Pericles?"

"The significant thing is that they were a slave-owning, patriarchal civilization. Their science they borrowed from the Egyptians, their art from the Nubians. We must be careful not to repeat their mistakes."

Diogenes was disappointed and appalled but replied in a respectful manner, "Do you not give Greece credit for their love of truth, beauty and freedom, for their development of scientific inquiry, for the introduction of democracy into the world?"

"Their truth was merely opinion, their beauty was simply the prejudices of dead white males and their freedom was a mockery. As for democracy there was no democracy for women."

A deep feeling of homesickness overcame Diogenes. He saw no reason to talk with someone who was proud of his ignorance and bigotry. "Are there any questions you would like to ask of me," Diogenes asked.

"No."

"Then thank you, and I shall leave after thanking the young lady for my coffee."

~~~~~~~~~~~~~~~~~~~~~~~~~~~

Diogenes

As he left he was pleasantly surprised to see the gardener as though he had been waiting for him, "Why, Mr. Gardener, it is a breath of fresh air to see you."

"Diogenes, have you found an educated man?"

"No, not one. The experience has dispirited me. I can now judge my own civilization with more understanding and compassion. The edge of my cynicism has been dulled. I have a great urge to return to Greece. If I can make the trip I swear I will never again be a cynic."

"If you have nowhere to stay tonight you can stay with me. It's not much. Mrs. Tolover has a room you can have for tonight two doors from mine. There is one bathroom on my floor. I can lend you a towel."

"You are very kind, sir."

"Have you eaten?"

"Not for a while."

"Then let's go, I'll buy you dinner."

"You are kind, generous and the one bright spot of my visit to this university. You have been considerate and helpful as well as learned. But the truth is I am apprehensive. You might say I am afraid. I don't know how I got here and I don't know how I might return home. It is home that I seek.

"I have a feeling that if I lie under the tree from which I awoke that I would somehow be transferred home. I would like to lie there now."

"Then can I bring you some dinner?"

"That would be most generous, thank you, for I am

hungry."

They walked across the campus to the tree. Diogenes sat on the ground, placed his lantern near to him and leaned against the tree.

"I will return in a few minutes. Do not leave this spot."

"I will not leave under my own power," Diogenes said as he stretched out on the ground.

The gardener walked away in the direction of a thoroughfare amid honking horns and murmuring engines, where, across the street the lights of several small businesses warmly glowed in the twilight.

He went in one of the fast-food restaurants and ordered two cheeseburgers, two orders of french fries and three small salads. The fragrance of the hot food wafted upward as he returned to the campus.

In a few minutes he approached the tree. He saw no one. *The tree must be hiding Diogenes, he thought.* But when he reached it Diogenes was gone. He stood looking around. Then he sat alone on the grass, took out one of the cheeseburgers and began eating.

~~~~~~~~~~~~~~~~~~~~~~~~~~~

"Why, there he is, lying under that tree," said Aristotle.

"My eyes are not as sharp as they once were," said Plato. "I'll take your word for it. My brooch has opened and loosened my chiton. They don't make

things as well as they used to. You go ahead, I'll fol-
low."

Happy relief showed on his face as Aristotle
approached his friend. "Where were you this morning, Diogenes. What happened?"

"Aristotle, you won't believe it. Where is Plato, is
he with you?"

"That new brooch he bought last week has failed.
There, I see him now, slowly he comes."

When he arrived Plato said, "Diogenes, it's good
you are not hurt. We were worried. Shall we walk as
we talk."

As the three friends walked Plato was the first to
speak, "Diogenes, as I get older I agree more and more
with your cynical attitude, especially about the merchants. You have more wisdom than I have previous-
ly given you credit for."

"He has something to tell us, Plato, let's listen to his
story."

"As I slept Hermes lifted me and carried me away.
He deposited me in a strange land, some far-off land
of the future. He placed me under a tree of an academy that they call a university. Everything around me
was new and different. A noisy chariot came towards
me that cut a swath in the grass and turned it into a
beautiful carpet of green. Yet that, the marvelous
lamps and a thing of magic called a phone that rings,
those are the only things I observed that were superi-

Carl Charbonnet

or to what we have in Athens today. The university, it appeared, does as much disucating as educating."

"Huh?" said Plato.

"Disucating," intoned Aristotle, "a word you picked up in the new land perhaps? Let me see if I can infer its meaning from what you said. If they don't educate, they disucate. If to educate is to engender morality, character and understanding, then to disucate must be to engender immorality, sleaze and misunderstanding."

"Very good, Aristotle." Diogenes continued, "Respect and compassion are still observed by a minority of those I met but wisdom seems to have vacated the academy. It did not take me long to determine an objective for my visit. I took my lighted lantern and sought to find an educated man at this prestigious university."

"Did you meet with any teachers?"

"Yes. It was easy to meet with them because they do not teach. They believe teaching undergraduates is beneath their dignity and a waste of time."

"Strange for teachers."

"What else did you learn from these 'teachers'?"

"Every teacher I spoke with showed contempt for his own land."

"Even the Corinthians do not go that far," said Aristotle, "the pride in their city state is enormous, though it is difficult to see what they have to be proud of."

Diogenes

"We Athenians have Persia to contend with," continued Diogenes, "They have something called the Environmental Protection Agency. I don't know what it is, but I can tell by the tone of arrogance of the teacher when he evoked the words Environmental Protection Agency, that it bodes poorly for those hapless people.

"They worship a god called Government who resides in a place called Washington, D.C."

"What does D.C. stand for?" asked Aristotle.

"My time there was so short that I was unable to find out., but they talked about D.C. with such reverence that I think it might mean Divine Cathedral.

"Their mythology tells them that Government can solve all their problems, even to the rearing of children and the elimination of poverty."

"It is difficult to understand people from a different age," said Plato.

"Extraordinary," said Aristotle. "What has this trip to the strange land taught you?"

"It has taught me that no society is nor can be perfect. It has cured me of cynicism. I know now that Athens is not as bad as I had thought. The adulation of government in the strange land has revealed to me new concepts. I have learned that human nature remains the same from age to age, that what is important is that civilization be constructed to best utilize that unchangeable nature. I see now that God, in his

Carl Charbonnet

infinite wisdom, designed man so that if left free and in peace he must serve others in order to satisfy his own needs. I can see now that the greed of the merchants is limited by the market itself, since to satisfy their greed they must first serve their customers. The greed of politicians and governmental bureaucrats is more difficult to limit as the connection between them is disconnected or obscured. Governments fail when they ignore nature and direct the lives of each of us by force."

"In your search at the university in the daytime with your lantern looking for an educated man, were you able to find any?"

"Yes, one," Diogenes responded, "The gardener."

ART

Gathered in the great New York auction house of Anerheim's were art dealers from New Orleans, collectors from London and buyers from museums around the world. Agents for the rich from Paris to Dallas occupied many seats.

A thirteenth-century Chinese vase went for $22,000. An Italian inlaid table from the seventeenth century sold for $9,000. A French porcelain figurine twelve inches high brought $2,000 per inch.

The murmur of the crowd stopped as everyone concentrated on the introduction of the centerpiece item, the DeLaHousé impressionist painting *Man of Character.*

Two assistants rolled it in on a wheeled table and positioned it to the left of the podium. The painting rested on crimson velvet. A white satin cloth covered the masterpiece. Patrons in the rear stretched their

Carl Charbonnet

necks to get a look. Patrons in the front row tingled with the realization of their privileged positions.

When the cloth was lifted, exposing the painting to view Oohs and Aahs filled the room.

Man of Character depicted a roughly dressed, man sitting on a low log. His deeply lined face exuded character. A life of toil showed in his gnarled hands. As patrons viewed the painting, the greatness of it evoked compassion for the toil the old man had suffered to earn such a face of character so well captured by DeLaHousé. They knew they were viewing greatness.

"*Man of Character*," began the auctioneer, "is so well-known it is redundant for me to point out its features. Let me say only that for more than a hundred years this painting has brought humankind together. The character of the man so powerfully portrayed by DeLaHousé inspires us all.

"May the bidding begin at $400,000."

The bidding quickly reached one million dollars. The price rose more slowly after that: "One million, one hundred thousand." "One million, one hundred-fifty thousand." "One million, one hundred-seventy thousand." It inched up until at one million, two hundred-thousand, it was sold. The room applauded as each turned to look at the purchaser. It was Ronnie Milleride, son of deceased billionaire John Milleride.

The patrons filed out.

Art

The purchaser, the gallery owner, the seller and the art critic for the *New York Courier-Ledger* formed their own group. It was just after noon when the purchaser invited the other three to lunch at the exclusive Club Escadrille.

In a mood of celebration they left the building to hail a cab from the curb in front of the gallery. The gallery owner hailed cabs from this exact place two or three times a week, but today it was different. An old man sat on the curb in just the spot the owner was accustomed to standing when he hailed a cab.

As the old man sat on the low curb, he pensively stared ahead. He was roughly dressed. His deeply lined face exuded character. A life of toil showed in his gnarled hands.

"What's that old man doing here?" shouted the seller.

"Move!" commanded the gallery owner.

"Why are those kind of people allowed around here?" asked the purchaser.

"Disgusting," pronounced the art critic.

WATER SHORTAGE

"We are so fortunate to have an Environmental Protection Agency to put people in jail and take their property, and an alert media to warn us of the national and international water shortage. Let me tell you what I read: Only one-third of one percent of all the water in the world is good for drinking without expensive processing."

"Yeah. And that one-third of one percent leaves only sixty billion gallons for every man, woman and child - born and unborn."

"And I have read that water, being a natural resource, is nonrecyclable and we are going to run out soon. The molecules or atoms get twisted or something, and we can't use it twice. Or maybe the electrons start going the other way around the nucleus, and if you drink it you get dizzy."

"Yeah, it's really terrible. And only 12,000 gallons

of water per day fall on the land area of the earth for every man woman and child every day. For a family of four that's only 48,000 gallons per day. Why, that would barely fill two good-size swimming pools. What are we going to do?"

"Yeah, and think of all the work to recycle the water."

"Yes, you have to look at the falling rain or at least hear it pattering on the roof, it's terrible."

"It is terrible. We are so fortunate to have an alert media and university community to warn us about such important things instead of wasting their time on trivialities such as a massive and growing government that no longer follows the Constitution."

"Yeah, who wants to hear about the government not following the rule of law when we can hear about running out of water?"

"I think we should conserve water, but not the Constitution."

"Yeah!"

ADIE

As they walked along the quay the smell of baking bread wafted from a small shop to their left. Next to the bakery was a jewelry and watch shop, then a women's clothing store and a few homes, all touching, and built right up to the quay. To their right, chug-chugging engines pushed heavy laden barges along the waterway.

"We need change," said Adie.

"*Watch out for that puddle!*" said Hilda. Adie was so engrossed in his thoughts he had failed to notice.

He glanced down, walked around the puddle, and then continued: "People are out of work. There are no jobs. The government is not doing enough to provide jobs. The individual worker is powerless against the great industrialist. The country must move to the left away from the bankers and greedy businessmen."

"That's good, Adie. You care. You want to do

something. But can you make any money in politics? Don't you have to get elected first?"

"Ah, Hilda, you're so naive. I'm interested in my country, in its people."

"That's good, most of the men I know are only interested in sex, having fun and making money.

"I like being with you, Adie. You don't have money now, but I can tell you'll do well in the future. I enjoy just walking down the quay with you. But this is the first time I've seen you in six weeks."

"Be grateful for each hour we spend together. That is all I can tell you."

"You like politics, don't you, Adie?"

"Yes. It's exciting. It makes the adrenaline flow. And I like the speeches. Did you know I had them spellbound last week?"

"Elen and all my other girlfriends are married now. Time is passing."

"Hilda, I don't think I'll be able to get married now. My work demands my full time. And what about your friend, Hans?"

"Hans is all right, but you're something special."

"Do you still see him?"

"Yes, we have a date tomorrow night."

~~~~~~~~~~~~~~~~~~~~~~~~~

It was a boisterous, happy place as Hans and Hilda enjoyed mugs of beer. They engaged in the group singing for awhile, and then began talking quietly to each other.

Hans began, "I don't approve of your friend Adie. I can't put my finger on it, but there's something sinister about him. I think he's dangerous."

"Oh! How can you say that? Adie is a fine man; he has principles and ambition. He's in politics; he's a spellbinding speaker. He'll make his mark some day real soon."

"I don't trust him. I don't think you should either."

"You're jealous, that's what it is. That's the only thing it could be."

"If he's so fine why doesn't he get a real job?"

"He's in politics and that's very important. Our country needs change, and he wants the government to do more. There is too much unemployment. People need jobs. Adie cares."

"If he cared for you, he would have asked you to marry him."

"He's very busy with his work but he's coming over Saturday night at eight o'clock. I'm going to introduce him to my mother and father. If he asks me to marry him, I'll say yes."

"You're throwing yourself at the wrong man. I tell you, Adie is no good."

Hilda stood up. "Take me home! We have nothing more to say."

~~~~~~~~~~~~~~~~~~~~~~~~~~

Carl Charbonnet

The knock on the door came promptly at eight o'clock. Hilda eagerly walked to the door and opened it. She took him by the hand and escorted him to the family room where her parents waited.

Standing before her parents she proudly said, "Father and Mother, this is my friend, Adolph Hitler."

WOODPECKER

A warm, gentle breeze barely rustled the leaves of the big oak tree. On the trunk and in the branches six woodpeckers were busy pecking.

Each woodpecker grabbed the bark with its sharp claws and climbed and pecked in search of moist, tasty insects.

Shirley noticed that Alphonse was having trouble. "Alphonse, what is the matter?"

"I don't know. It is hard for me to hold on to the side of the tree. And when I peck it hurts my beak, it seems like my eyes are going to fall out, and the whole thing gives me a headache."

Harry flew down, perched on a nearby branch and said, "What's going on here?"

"It's Alphonse," said Shirley. "It is hard for him to hold onto the side of the tree and when he pecks, it hurts his beak, and it feels like his eyes are going to fall out and it all gives him a headache."

"Well, let me show him how." Harry took his place next to Alphonse. "Grab the bark like this," he said as his sharp claws bit deeply into the bark making him secure.

Alphonse copied the movement but his claws just went in a little, not enough to hold him and he fell off. He flapped his wings frantically and flew back up next to Harry. Again he tried, clawing the bark as hard as he could. This time he was able to hold on and so he began pecking. Sharp pain shot through his neck and head, so he stopped.

"What's the matter now?" said Harry.

"It just hurts so much," he said trembling.

"Get hold of yourself, Alphonse," boomed Harry. "Be a woodpecker, man. I never heard of a wood-pecker who didn't like giving a tree a good, hard peck. Give it another try."

Alphonse tried again evoking this comment from Harry, "No wonder. You're not doing it right. You're not using your tail feathers. Brace yourself with your tail feathers like this," he said as he firmly pushed his tail feathers against the tree then gave it a vigorous peck. "You see now? Try it that way."

Alphonse braced himself with his tail feathers; as he did the tips of the feathers broke off and fluttered down to the ground. But he tried again and again, faster and faster until the pain became so unbearable he fell off the tree all the way to the ground. He lay on the ground exhausted and shaking.

Shirley and two other birds flew down to him. "We must take him to Aristotle, the owl. He will know what to do," said Fred.

"Yes," said Shirley, "I think he is terribly sick."

Alphonse stirred and got to his feet. His head still hurt and he was dizzy.

"Alphonse," said Shirley, "We think you should see Aristotle, the owl. He will know what to do."

"Yes. All right. I can fly now."

Slowly they flew over the mountain, across the valley and to the next mountain top. "Do you think he will be home?" asked Shirley.

"Yes," said Fred. "He stays home in the daytime."

So they got an audience with Aristotle the wise owl. "What seems to be the trouble?" said Aristotle.

"It's Alphonse," said Shirley. "He has a terrible headache."

"Well, let him speak. Alphonse, do you want to tell me what the trouble is?"

"Yes, sir.

"All the other woodpeckers fly up to a tree and grab onto the side of it and hold on like it is nothing. With me it's difficult and sometimes I fall off. When I do get a good enough hold and start pecking it hurts my beak, it feels like my eyes will fall out and I get a headache."

"Well, of course you do."

Carl Charbonnet

"What do you mean, sir, 'Of course I do,'?"

"Because you're not a woodpecker. You're a mocking bird."

"I am!" said a relieved Alphonse. "That must be why I have never been content to just chirp the same notes but always wanted to sing many different songs; why I always wanted to imitate every beautiful song I hear."

"Exactly right. Forget about pecking trees. Do what you were born to do. Go about singing. I haven't heard a good song in the forest for some time. I'll be looking forward to hearing you sing from now on. Do you know, Carry Me Back To Old Virgini?"

"No sir. Could you hum a few bars?"

"Owls don't hum."

"That's O K. In the past I've heard some of the best popular singers and greatest operas. This wonderful music has been bursting inside of me trying to get out."

"Well, whatever you decide to sing, I'll be listening. Be off with you."

After thanking the wise owl three or four more times Alphonse and his friends flew off and returned to their flock and the big oak tree.

The woodpeckers flew this way then that until they each had found a spot on the tree's trunk. Alphonse took his position on a high limb. He could hardly wait to begin singing. With his shortened tail feathers behind him and his chest thrust out in front he began. His clear notes spread down to the forest floor where

Woodpecker

rabbits stopped hopping and field mice stopped scur-
rying as they listened to the beautiful music. A high
flying eagle heard the faint but beautiful sound and
dived to get closer. He soared one time around, then
took his position on the highest branch of the tallest
tree. One by one Alphonse's friends, the woodpeckers, stopped pecking as all listened to him as he sang
a medley beginning with Frank Sinatra's My Way,
then John Tesh at Red Rocks. Then he went on to two
Mozart Études and finished with Marguerite's final
aria from Charles Gounod's Faust - Angels Pure,
Angels Radiant.

THE PILGRIMS

The established Church of England was pervasive. The Government and the Church worked together to oppress other churches.

And many Christians objected to the Church's departure from biblical principles. They said the Church's doctrine was not pure enough. Some of these Puritans set up small, independent churches. One such church took their religion so seriously that they left the country to find religious freedom. Members moved by ship to the Netherlands and settled in Leyden.

Problems arose and they were not happy there. They decided to venture to the New World, start from scratch and build a colony in the wilderness of America. Nothing would deter them from following their convictions and practicing their religion in freedom.

A group of London businessmen headed by

Carl Charbonnet

Thomas Weston agreed to finance the trip. Filled with optimism the Puritans met with Weston to discuss the agreement.

"You agree then," said John Carver, "To buy us a ship and pay for our supplies. In return we are to load the ship with lumber and other produce, sail back to Europe and deliver the cargo to you."

"Yes, we do so agree," replied Weston.

Robert Cushman broke in, "Mr. Weston, how about medical insurance?"

"Medical insurance? What's that?"

"It means that you will provide us with doctors, medicine and hospital care when needed."

"Doctors, medicine and hospital care. I've never heard of anything like that. Where did you get that idea?"

"We are bringing our families with us, our wives and children. There will be babies born. In the New World we might encounter wild animals. Indigenous people are a threat. Perhaps unknown diseases will strike us down. We might injure ourselves as we engage in cutting trees and other hard work. Until we build houses we might suffer from exposure. We must have full medical coverage."

"We are willing to risk this investment for you, but you have gone too far. Medical insurance, as you express it, is out of the question."

So the Pilgrims withdrew. That is why the Pilgrims did not come to the New World.

QUALITY OF LIFE

Professor Jim Smith held the chair of Peace and Love at prestigious Bovundy University.

He was not an ordinary professor. So great was his reputation that each day when he walked from his car in the parking lot to his office, he was pointed out by students and faculty. "Why there goes Professor Smith," one student would say to his companion, who might reply, "Wow! it really is."

His reputation extended beyond Bovundy: The textbooks he authored are in use at 157 colleges and universities in America and the universities of nine foreign countries.

His widely quoted books, articles and lectures have made him the intellectual leader of the euthanasia movement in America. He is the unchallenged authority. *Euthanasia* is his most widely quoted book. Perhaps the most quoted passage is from page 219:

Carl Charbonnet

"Euthanasia is the kindest manifestation of a caring people." On page 234 he says, "When someone has outlived his usefulness, it is to the advantage of both that person and society that he depart gracefully and with dignity."

In another of his influential books, *Quality of Life*, Professor Smith delineates, with a surgeon's precision, the nature and meaning of quality of life. The book begins with the conclusion that the proper choice with regard to unwanted babies is abortion. "Already," Professor Smith writes, "over thirty million babies have been saved from the disappointments of life. Abortion is the true pro-life position." He goes on to describe which babies are unwanted. "It would be cruel to bring into the world a baby with a severe mental or physical defect," he says in Chapter 13. In Chapter 15 he says, "New specialties must be taught in medical schools so that we will have a trained group of doctors who will know which babies, as well as which adults, should be helped by euthanasia."

In Chapter 2 he slays, "We can all thank a wise Supreme Court which, on January 22, 1973, did not let a mere 'oath of office to uphold the Constitution' prevent them from giving women the right of freedom of choice concerning their own bodies. The famous Roe vs. Wade decision was so progressive it should be celebrated as a national holiday. But that's not all. The

Quality of Life

lower courts and some legislatures had compassion for those women who, under extreme stress of an unwanted pregnancy, were unable to quickly make up their minds. For these women the time of legal abortion was extended so that today more than 10,000 women terminate their pregnancies in the third trimester in clean, hospital conditions." He decrees in Chapter 20, "An enlightened society is one where we are bold enough to throw traditional morality out the window and do the right thing."

Quality of Life had become the nation's authority on all questions concerning euthanasia.

His reputation and popularity had been enhanced by his close association with the future First Lady, Margery Randall Miller, with whom he shared views. The evening news had shown them together many times advocating various new governmental programs. He admired Margery Miller's advocacy for the empowerment of small children to sue their parents. After all, what right did parents have to force their son or daughter to study or to refuse them the use of the family car? When she came out for universal government supported child care, he publicly called her one of the most intelligent people America has ever produced. When her husband had become President she had immediately organized a secret conference of left-wing extremists to plan a medical program for the nation. The meeting had been closed to the public, the

Carl Charbonnet

medical profession and the insurance industry.
Margery had wanted no impediment for a quick
takeover of one-seventh of the nation's economy. The
completed document contained more than 800 coercive
words, words like "fine" and "imprisonment."
Professor Smith had said, "What a wonderful lady.
She is going to be sure that everybody obeys her
orders. Little people are jealous of her power - that's
the only reason they don't like her: they can't stand a
powerful woman."

President Bob Miller knew the popularity of the
great Professor Jim Smith. He wanted to do the right
thing. He urged Congress to enact legislation man-
dating euthanasia. His party held the majority and
there were few among them who opposed the idea.

But there was a sticking point: how to decide which
people had such a low quality of life that they could be
better served by terminating their misery. Consider
this: When low-quality people are no longer with us,
the average quality of life will be higher.

President Miller, the great American President of
Change, exercised his leadership. He proposed to
Congress that a Cabinet-level Department of Quality
of Life be created and that the Secretary be given the
power to decide who would be selected for beneficent
euthanasia. The law was enacted. President Miller
nominated the renowned Professor Jim Smith as
Secretary of Quality of Life.

Quality of Life

Prior to this, Professor Smith had been on a speaking tour at a flat fee of $40,000 for each lecture. So greedy was he for this money that he accepted all requests to speak, sometimes as many as three a day in three different cities. One day, after traveling and working for forty-eight days without stopping, he felt exhausted and barely made it to his hotel room. Too tired even to lock the door behind him, he stumbled to a soft chair and fell into it.

As he sat trying to relax, it suddenly hit him. He felt tingling over most of his body. He felt he was no longer in charge of himself. Fear gripped him. As he tried to rise from the chair, he fell to the floor. He was having a stroke.

As he lay on the floor he found his left leg didn't work. He could not move it. He tried to touch his left leg with his left hand. He couldn't nor could he move his left arm. He moved his right leg. It worked. He tried his right arm. He could move it but not well. He wondered at the quietness. He looked at the TV and realized it was on and had been on, but he heard no sound. He tried to shout but could not talk. In a blinding flash, words from Chapter 24 of *Euthanasia* came to him: "When considering the two legs, two arms, speech, hearing and sight, if a person has less than fifty percent of these faculties he or she should be considered a candidate for euthanasia." He shivered at this revelation.

I can shiver, he thought as though addressing a court, *That should be added to my capabilities. And I can think. Won't these two abilities raise my capabilities above fifty percent?*

I can't be seen like this. What can I do? I'll get Harry.

His assistant, Harry, was in the adjacent room. Professor Smith dragged himself along the floor to the wall separating the two rooms and hit it with his fist. He knew it wasn't a strong enough blow. He was able to take off one shoe. He took it by the toe and hit the wall with the heel as hard as he could. *Surely Harry heard that,* he thought.

Harry knocked. He knocked again. Then he entered. On the floor was the professor writing on hotel stationery placed on a phone book. He had started with regular-sized letters, but his control was so bad the letters were illegible. Now he was writing in letters two inches high. When finished they said, "HOSPITAL - DON'T TELL - INCOGNITO - INCOGNITO."

Harry successfully got him to the nearest hospital, then transferred him to a hospital in the Caribbean where he was put under a doctor's care under the assumed name of Albert Jocaster Springfellow.

When his Cabinet appointment was received at the university it was forwarded, by computer, to another Professor Jim Smith.

Quality of Life

That Jim Smith was not well-known except by a group of other professors hostile to his outdated ideas of limited government and family values. He had a reputation of being uncaring, old-fashioned and standing in the way of progress. They wondered how such a man had slipped in after their years of effort to keep such people off the campus. They had been studying how to get him fired. Therefore they were glad for this opportunity to get rid of him and so did not say anything that would reveal the truth.

The Senate was so enamored of the reputation of the first Professor Smith that they perfunctorily approved him without a hearing.

At his arrival at the White House the president stretched out his hand in greeting. "Professor Smith, at last I am meeting one of my favorite people and by all measures the smartest man in America. It is a distinct pleasure."

As they took seats in the Oval Office the President continued, "Jim, may I call you Jim?"

"Of course, Mr. President."

"As Secretary of the Department of Quality of Life, you have been empowered to decide which Americans will be selected to receive the benefit of euthanasia. You have been granted plenipotentiary powers.

"The reason you have this position and these powers is because of me. I put you there. Do you get my drift?"

Carl Charbonnet

"I think so, Mr. President."

"Call me Bob."

"Yes, Bob, I understand you."

"Then I have a, er, request."

"Of course."

"The opinion polls tell me that this is a popular thing. My advisors tell me the American people want change and they want the Department of Quality of Life to make changes.

"This is my baby, and I want the credit. Here is what I have in mind.

"We would introduce this entire effort at a joint session of the House of Representatives and the Senate on prime-time TV, with all the networks broadcasting it. I would say a few words and introduce you.

"My public relations advisors tell me it would make the greatest impact if you personally on that day select two people, whom you have arranged to have in the chamber, to be the first two selected for the honor of euthanasia."

"I see no problem."

"Good. Then it's settled. How much time do you need?"

"Two months."

"Can you make it forty days."

"If you wish."

Professor Smith got to work. Diligently he searched for the two most appropriate candidates in all the country for euthanasia. The criteria for these two people required that they would be leading such a low quality of life that the decision to help them leave life with dignity would be accepted by the vast majority of Americans.

The White House had no trouble making a media event out of the joint session at which Secretary Smith would make his decision known. The date was decided and the time was set for 9 p.m. Eastern, 6 p.m. Pacific time, to reach the largest audience.

Legislators filed in the House chamber and took their seats. All nine Justices of the Supreme Court took their seats in the front row. The 435 Representatives and 100 Senators took their seats. Distinguished visitors and famous people filled all remaining seats. When the President and Margery Randall Miller entered hand in hand, the assembled people roared with adulation. Most gave a standing ovation. They knew that here was a President who was really bringing change, just as he had promised.

Margery Randall Miller took a seat of honor as the President went to the podium. While he waited for the applause to die down he looked around to see if he could spot the two selectees. He saw an elderly lady in a wheelchair. *That must be one,* he thought as he gave her his most ingratiating smile, the one that said, "Don't worry, I care, I'll solve your problems for you."

Carl Charbonnet

Then he spoke, "We are entering a new age of enlightenment. Tonight we throw off the shackles of superstition that have kept us from reaching our full potential. Under my leadership the Congress and Senate have created a new Department, the Department of Quality of Life. I have nominated and the Senate has approved Professor Jim Smith of Bovundy University." Another standing ovation for the professor.

"Secretary Smith has been given the power to improve the quality of Life in America. He has been working assiduously to find the first two candidates that our beneficent government will assist to exit this life with dignity.

"Secretary Smith has told me that those two candidates are in this chamber now. He will give their names. I have instructed my Secret Service to assist the Sergeant at Arms to escort the two candidates from the chamber. In case there is some misunderstanding, they have been instructed to escort them whether or not they realize the benefits of being selected. To you two selectees, let me offer a personal remark. You are pioneers. Your names will go down in history as we kick off the change we all seek, the change I promised you.

"Secretary Smith, the podium is yours."

Some people in the front rows were bewildered because they did not recognize this Professor Jim

Smith. But most were unaware of the switch of the Jim Smiths and applauded loudly.

After the applause died down Secretary Smith began, "Fellow Americans, I have been given an awesome responsibility.

"Ever since my nomination I have studied this difficult challenge.

"We all agree that human compassion requires that people incapable of enjoying a high quality of life should be saved from their torture by euthanasia.

"The initial assignment given to me by the President was to identify the two Americans with the lowest quality of life. Arrangements have been made to assist these two selectees to terminate their lives in dignity.

"What is quality of life? What is the lack of it?

"It is said that physical disability characterizes lack of quality. The most frequent example given is a child born with Down's syndrome. Such people cannot enjoy life and are no good to anyone else, it has been said. I have read that in many papers written by our wisest scholars and published in the university presses and scholarly journals.

"As for myself I have known children with Down's syndrome who have lived at home with their loving parents. The parents I know have led rich and fulfilling lives. Some credit their afflicted child with enriching their lives.

Carl Charbonnet

"Charles DeGaulle, as a World War II leader, refused to accept defeat by the Nazis even after they occupied his country. When he fled to organize the Free French, his former friends in the French Vichy government put a death sentence on his head. In the face of these obstacles, Charles DeGaulle prevailed. By understanding and great character he saved France three times and gave to the world an extraordinary example of character. Richard Nixon said of him, 'The clarity of his vision allowed him to recognize the great movements of history while others could only see the events of the day.'

"Charles DeGaulle had a child born with Down's syndrome. He and Mrs. DeGaulle loved, adored and nurtured the child. DeGaulle said that his interaction with his daughter Anne had given him insights and taught him lessons. He said the experience with his beloved Anne had strengthened his character and enabled him to defy the world and stand firm for right against wrong. Today I cannot recommend any innocent child afflicted with Down's syndrome for euthanasia. I was forced to look further to fill the spots.

"Many studies by distinguished professors have proven that old people are useless. They suffer from bad backs, arthritic fingers; some can barely walk across the room. We must stop their suffering, I have read. My own experience is that for fifteen years I have met with the ladies at Saint Martin's in the Pines on Saturday nights. Some of them have sharp and clear minds; some have minds diminished by age to various degrees. All are precious. I had to look beyond old people to find the two selectees I will announce tonight.

"As I studied the challenge given me by my President I wondered, 'What constitutes low quality of life and what constitutes high quality of life?'

"High quality of life is based on goodness, understanding and accomplishments. Goodness is founded in the heart; understanding comes from experience, opinions, prejudices and reasoning; accomplishments are manifest in the maintenance and improvement of the human condition. A good person will be concerned for moral principles and for other people from conception to and through old age. One with understanding knows that the government cannot solve our problems and will take responsibility for his actions and work to solve his own problems. As he has the strength to do so, he will help others who are in need. A good person will tell the truth. A good person will be faithful to his or her spouse. A good person will live by principle and not expediency.

"Someone with low quality of life is not concerned with the truth or with fidelity to his spouse. He lacks principle - he says what he perceives his listeners want to hear and changes his position to accommodate the prejudices of the day. His desires are unimpeded by morality.

"He does not care for the most helpless Americans,

the babies residing in their mothers' wombs. He has no respect for the sanctity of life from conception to and through old age. If married, he will commit adultery at every opportunity. He will prevaricate to get what he wants, whether it is money or political power. If he also lacks understanding, he will vote for that politician who will promise to solve his problems. The only thing more harmful to society than such a greedy voter is the politician himself who exploits voter greed and frenetically works to enact more laws, more regulations, more taxes as he tells the people he is doing it for them. This combination of personal immorality and statist impulses describes the lowest quality of life that can be found.

"The two people my studies have shown to suffer from the lowest quality of life in America and whose euthanasia will raise the average quality of life the most will be announced now. I have selected President Bob Miller and Margery Randall Miller.

"Sergeant at Arms, do your duty."

THE FIRST WORD

THE INVENTION OF LANGUAGE

I'm a shy sort of a guy. It's real hard for me to meet girls.

Once I meet them I'm all right, but meeting them is difficult at best.

It was registration day at the university. I hate registration, which is mostly standing in line all day. But I had to go through with it and so I stood in line. There were four lines. I got in the second one.

With nothing else to do my eyes aimlessly went to the right, to the first person in the third line, then moved back down the line. At about the sixth or seventh person, my head involuntarily jerked back to the girl standing third in line. She looked clean and fresh like she dew glistening on the leaves of green grass struck by the first rays of the sun. I couldn't take my eyes off her. I saw the way her soft, brown hair framed her face. I looked at her left shoulder and arm.

Carl Charbonnet

My eyes dwelled on her trim waist. The way her skirt wrapped around her revealed not the modish gaunt body of a model, but a real shapely woman. Below the mid-knee hemline of her skirt I was excited to see the large, shapely curves of a dancer.

We were taught in Anatomy 202 that all synapses were located in the brain, but I think for me, they were sparking tingling all over my body. *I have to meet her! I must meet her!*

But how?

My line moved forward a little. Now I was almost even with her. She was just four feet away. What was I to do? Should I say something? Could I say something?

I've watched those guys who find it easy to talk to a girl they've never met before or even been introduced to. If somebody introduced us I could talk. My insides were agitated and my voice seemed frozen at the same time.

Then she reached the head of the line. *Would I lose her when she left?* Then I reached the head of my line. I was even with her. I could have touched her on the shoulder, I was that close. I still couldn't think of anything to say. She was looking down at the papers on the table, then looking up to the registration clerk. Then I saw her card showing the courses she already had chosen. I was able to read one - History of Language 101 - when someone interrupted me.

The Invention of Language

"Huh, what?" I fumbled to my registration clerk.

"What elective do you want?"

I looked down at my note where I had written the name of the elective course I had decided on - Computer Circuits and Applications 303 - then looked up and blurted out - "History of Language 101."

~~~~~~~~~~~~~~~~~~~~~~~~~~~~

I had not seen her since registration time. The first day of class found me in the hallway outside the classroom early, tense and trying to look calm.

As I waited a friend approached, "Hey Keith. Are you in this class?"

"Yeah, I am."

"Well, come and sit with me."

"I have to finish smoking."

"But you don't have a cigarette."

"Do you have a cigarette, George?"

"No. You know I don't smoke. And I don't think you do either. Hey, are you . . . "

George was still talking when I saw her coming. My ears went deaf and my mind went numb. She was holding her books in front of her like girls do and walking like girls do. She walked right past me and into the classroom with me following like a zombie. When she sat down, I sat down - right next to her. I stared ahead because that's all I was able to do. Then without knowing what I would say I slowly turned my

Carl Charbonnet

head in her direction. She looked at me and said, "Hi. I'm Jean Perrault."

That made it Okay for me as I said, "Hi, I'm Keith Russell."

That was a class I'll remember all my life. Of course I had no idea what the professor said, I haven't a clue, but that's all right. Jean had made notes. That gave me an excuse to phone her and ask for her help.

I asked her to bring her notes and we'd go to Wunkie's Burger House and get coffee and talk. It was midafternoon and we were the only customers there. I sat on one side of the table, Jean on the other.

She must be a fast writer, or conversant in short-hand, or something because she had extensive notes. This is what her notes said, this is exactly what she had written down as the professor lectured:

> Today I will tell you of one of the greatest accomplishments of all history.

> Before China, before Egypt, Israel, Babylon, and Sumer there was Basabur. Basabur prospered 7,000 years ago in Mesopotamia. In the year 7,000 B.C. there was no language anywhere in the world.

> Private citizens didn't know what to do. They were grunting and howling and generally bumping into each other. So the democratic government of Basabur established a Department for the Invention of Language.

The Invention of Language

The best and the brightest were selected for this important work. The Secretary of the Department for the Invention of Language was a Mr. Dunnly Ur, one of the best educated men in Basabur. He organized a commission.

"You have been selected," said Secretary Ur to the members of the commission, "because each of you has distinguished himself in some particular way. The invention of language is an awesome task. I will begin by saying that we cannot have a language until we have grammar."

"Owah, owah," they agreed in unison.

"The most fundamental parts of grammar are subject and verb. You can't have a sentence without a subject and a verb."

"What's a sentence?" asked one.

"Does anyone know what a sentence is?"

"Is that the same as an elbow?"

"No, not at all."

"Anybody else want to try?"

"Well," said a thoughtful member, "If sentence is not an elbow, maybe it means knee."

"Wrong again. Let me explain. A sentence is a part of language. It consists of two or more words."

"What's a word?"

"A word is the smallest part of language. Verb is a word. Sentence is a word. Elbow is a word."

"Is there a word for everything?"

"Well, not yet. That's why were here. That is our work, to invent words for everything. Then we will combine the words into sentences and then we will have language."

One commissioner stood up, "Is there a word for . . . " as he spoke he held his hands high in front of himself, palms facing each other. He rolled his eyes as he moved his hands down, in and out in smoothly suggestive curves.

"Wwwwooooooo . . . " sounded the assemblage in unison.

"You've just spoken. You've just invented a new word, 'wwwooo.'"

"I like that word. The next time I see a wwwooo I'll know what to say to get her attention. I can just see it now man, 'Hey wwwooo, come here, I want to talk with you.'"

"I think something so important should have more sounds that just wwwooo," said another.

"You mean more syllables," said Secretary Ur.

"More syllables, as you call the sounds."

"Any suggestions?"

"Well," said the man with the expressive hands, "My two favorite sounds, after grrr, are: hey and man. How about wwwooohey?"

"Well, I don't know."

"How about wwwoooman," said another.

"Now that's better. But it is too long. After we invent language we're going to have to invent writing and it will be easier if there are fewer letters. Let me suggest 'woman.'"

"Good, very good."

"All in favor of 'woman' to mean - and he made the curving motion with his hands - say aye."

There was a preponderance of ayes. "The ayes have it. Gentlemen, we have a beginning, our first word. Let's all retire for refreshments."

~~~~~~~~~~~~~~~~~~~~~~~~~~

Sitting opposite from Jean was great, as she read I looked into her face. Then she added, "It is not in my notes, but at the end the professor said, 'Just as today the Federal government is our great leader, benefactor and provider so was the national government of Basabur 7,000 years ago. Just imagine,' he had concluded, 'if it hadn't been for the national government of Basabur we would have no language today.'"

I stood up, walked around the table to Jean, bent down and kissed her on her mouth.

ROBBERS

John Fuller found college easy. Studying was effortless. But he preferred to play pool, drink beer with his buddies and date pretty girls. Even after government grants, college was expensive, and he ran out of money. So John dropped out and got a job with a small company that assembled computers.

Assembling computers wasn't the type of work he liked. His mind wandered. One day he realized he could make more money if he took home one or two computers and sold them to his former classmates at college. After the sixth such theft, he was caught and fired.

He left the company and aimlessly walked down the street with his hands in his pockets. He went into a local bar and ordered a beer. As he began his third bottle, he found himself talking with two other guys. It became a convivial group, one with red hair, one with blond and the third with brown. Each guy weighed within five pounds of 150 and was nearly exactly five foot ten inches. They all lived nearby and liked the local football team.

As the waitress brought rounds of beer, each would offer to pay until Max said, "I'm clean."

The time came when Chuck said, "That finishes me."

Later John said, "This is going to be the last," as he fished in his pocket for change.

"John, me and Chuck have a proposition for you. We know where we can get some money real quick, tonight."

"Oh?"

"You want a be in?"

"Why not."

So the three men robbed a gas station. They split the $117 three ways.

"Hey, let's get another beer," said Max.

"Not for me," said John, "I'm bushed."

They exchanged phone numbers and promised to get together real soon.

And they did get together again. Together they robbed four more gas stations and three Seven-Eleven stores. They became close friends. When John was evicted from his apartment and Chuck invited him to move in with him free of charge, he did.

One night after robbing a man and his wife returning to their car from a concert, Chuck said, "How much did we get tonight?"

"Sixty-nine dollars."

"That's not much. How much did we get all last week?"

"I believe it came to $400."

"Split three ways, that's not much for a week. We're as sorry-ass robbers as I've ever heard of."

"What can we do?"

"We can be smart thieves," said John. "Let me explain it this way: In the old days in Merrie Olde England, when a traveler went north from London he risked highwaymen coming out from the heath and the brambles and threatening him with guns and taking his watch and his money.

"Today the smart thief is the plaintiff's attorney. He's educated. He steals more and risks less. He manipulates the so called justice system, and the force of the sheriff's gun for his own enrichment. And the police can't touch him.

"Last week I read about a plaintiff's attorney who made over a million dollars in one lawsuit. And it was frivolous."

"What does frivolous mean?"

"In this case it means there was no merit. A man was painting his house on the weekend and fell off the ladder. He sued the maker of the ladder."

"You mean the ladder broke and he fell on his ass?"

"No, the ladder didn't break. He leaned over too far to one side and the ladder went over."

"But that wasn't the ladder's fault."

"That's what I like about it. The justice system has become unjust. I want to exploit the unjust justice system. A sap does a dumb thing and hurts himself and the court orders the ladder maker to pay him more than a hundred gas station robbers make in a lifetime."

"But I thought we had trial by jury. No reasonable jury would go along with that."

"Chuck, you hit the nail on the head. You get an unreasonable jury, the judge leans over backwards to help you."

"Huh?"

"This is the way it works if you're a crooked, big time lawyer like I want to be. You hire one or two special psychologists who help you screen the jurors. Then you strike, or get rid of, the capable ones – the ones who are capable of reasonable thought. What you are left with are twelve bimbos. Then you just go about posing, lying and moralizing and it usually works."

"I didn't know that," said Max. "That's cool."

"This lawyering business sounds better all the time," said Chuck.

"Look guys," said John, "Tonight we stole sixty-seven dollars and risked our freedom doing it. That lawyer stole three million, and the beauty of thing is he did not go to jail. They aren't even looking for him. He belongs to the country club, plays golf, wears snappy clothes, owns an Olympic-size pool, has six cars and TV makes him into a hero. That's what I call a smart thief."

"And what kind of lawyer did you say he was?"

"A plaintiff's attorney, the guy who initiates the suit. Other lawyers are saps who don't make in ten years what a plaintiff's attorney, dedicated to stealing money, makes in one case. Why there is a lawyer in Texas who took in more money in one case than a hundred decent lawyers make in a lifetime holding civilization together."

"Yeah, but we're not lawyers. We can't sue nobody."

"Look, I've been to college," said John. "I'm good at it. I got passing grades without hardly studying."

"So?" said Chuck.

"I left college because I ran out of money."

"Go on," said Max.

"If you guys would support me while I get my law degree, then when I start scooping in the money, I'll split it three ways."

"Doesn't it take a long time to get a law degree?"

"With the college credit I already have, I think I can do it in four years or less."

"That's a long time."

"Look at it this way. The way things are going, what are you going to be doing four years from now?"

"I don't know," said Max.

"I never thought about it," said Chuck.

"Well I'll tell you. You'll still be robbing gas stations for peanuts hoping to get a big score. When you stick your knife in the night clerk's ribs or point your handgun in the face of the gas station attendant and he hands over his roll of bills, it makes you feel good. But a large roll of ones is only a hundred, and if a roll is full of tens and twenties, it still is less than a thousand. I'm talking about a million for one case. Split three ways that's more than you can steal the old-fashioned way in a lifetime."

"And you would split with us three ways if we put you through college?"

"Yeah."

"And after you get your law degree we can retire?"

"That's right."

"But suppose we get caught and land in jail?"

"I'll be a lawyer, remember. I'll get you out."

"I'll drink to that," said Max.

"Then it's a deal?"

"It's a deal."

~~~~~~~~~~~~~~~~~~~~~~~~~~~~

John Fuller enrolled in college and paid the tuition with the combined funds of the three friends. Immediately he applied himself to his studies and did well, getting only A's and B's. As he got the hang of it and moved on to law school, his grades became straight A's.

The friends met regularly . Max and Chuck would talk about their latest robberies and hand over most of the money to sustain John.

Robbers

One night two and a half years later, Max met John alone. "Chuck has been arrested; I got away. Chuck's like you; he won't squeal on me."

"What are your plans, Max?"

"I don't know, I'm scared. I don't want to go to jail."

"What went wrong?"

"Nothing. We did what we have always done, but this time a guy with a cellular phone in his car saw us and called police. A patrol car was two blocks away."

"How did you get away?"

"Chuck was driving. He stopped and told me to get out so that only he was caught. I walked away and saw the patrol car racing after Chuck."

"Do you have the nerve to keep on by yourself?"

"I don't think so. I was thinking about getting a job. But I wouldn't be able to give you as much as we have been giving."

"Don't worry. I can get a loan for the difference. I don't have too much longer to go, and then the money will roll in."

~~~~~~~~~~~~~~~~~~~~~~~~~~~~~

John and Max continued to meet periodically. Max would tell him about the job he had in a gas station they had robbed two years before. Max did his shopping at the Salvation Army store so he could turn over more money to John. He would hand over as much money as he had after paying for bare necessities.

Eventually John graduated, received his Juris Doctorate, passed the bar exam and became a lawyer. In law school he had learned who the major plaintiff's attorney firms were, and he secured a job with one of them. Immediately he was given small cases and did well in the courtroom. He made a good living from the start.

One night Max went to their regular meeting place at the regular time but John was not there. He waited, drinking beer for four hours. John did not show up.

He phoned him but John had moved.

It took some effort, but Max finally learned where John was working and went to his office. "Do you have an appointment?" asked the receptionist.

"No, just tell him it is Max, he'll see me."

The receptionist left. In two minutes she reappeared, "Mr. Fuller is tied up on an important case right now. He asked if you could come back another day."

Shocked, Max didn't know what to say. He stared. The receptionist repeated, "Mr. Fuller is busy now, can you come back?"

"Did you personally tell him Max wanted to see him?"

"Yes."

Max slowly turned and left.

The next day he dialed the company from a pay phone.

"Who may I say is calling?"

"Max."

Robbers

"One moment please." Then, "I'm sorry, Mr. Fuller is out. Would you like to leave a message?"

"Yeah, tell him to meet me at the regular place Thursday, eight o'clock."

"I'll see that he gets the message."

But John did not show up at eight o'clock. Max waited until 9:30 and then left, somewhat depressed.

~~~~~~~~~~~~~~~~~~~~~~~~~~

Chuck's parole hearing came up. He was granted parole. Max met him at the prison entrance. They went to their regular place and ordered two beers.

"You look none the worse for where you've been."

"Thanks, I feel great today. It's a wonderful feeling to be out. How's John doing?"

"There is a problem, Chuck. He stood me up. He moved. He has a job with a swanky law firm. He won't see me."

"Won't see you!"

"That's right. He won't talk with me."

"Do you know where he lives now?"

"No, but I know where he works."

"Have you been there?"

"Yeah and I can't get through the receptionist. She says he is busy."

"And he knows it is you who wants to see him?"

"He knows."

"Then he might do the same to me."

"I expect so."

"I'll have to try."

The next day Chuck went to John's office and was told that 'Mister' Fuller was busy.

Chuck was enraged when he and Max next talked, "I don't like this. I don't like it at all. Here I take the rap and we both pay for his school and now that he has made it, he cuts us off."

"What can we do?"

"We'll catch him when he leaves work."

They spent two days learning that he did not come out the front door of the building because he parked in the basement garage. The next day they went to the garage at 4:30 and waited.

At 6:15 a man came through the elevator door. Max said, "There he is."

They both walked toward him. When John saw them he cheerily said, "Hey fellas. I've been thinking about you."

"John, we want to talk with you. Where can we go?"

John pushed up his sleeve as he looked down at his watch, "I'm sorry fellas, I'm late already. Let's make it some other time."

Chuck swung fast and hit John hard in the stomach. The punch doubled John over. He backed up holding his midsection.

He stayed that way for some time while he caught his breath. When he straightened up he had a gun in his hand and was pointing it at Chuck, "Okay, you guys. I'll say this once. I'm a lawyer now. I know what the law is and how to make it work for me. I don't want to see either of you ever again. If you try to contact me, Chuck, you'll be back in the slammer so fast you won't have time to put your pants on. And Max, I know what you've been doing. I have enough information on you to put you away for ten, maybe twenty years."

The two men backed up. They looked beaten. John smirked. He confidently put his gun away. He turned to walk to his car and kept talking, "You dumb creeps, you should be grateful for the time we spent together. I'm in the big ..."

Like a wild animal Chuck lunged at John this time striking him hard in the back of the neck. John fell. Max moved in and kicked him in the side of the head. They both stomped him.

"Hey, what are you doing there?" came a loud voice as two well-dressed men exited the elevator.

Max and Chuck ran.

The two men went to John and crouched down, "He's hurt badly."

"I think he's dead."

"We've witnessed a murder."

"Hey, isn't this that new plaintiff's attorney who just began his career with that shyster law firm on the seventh floor?"

"Yes, I believe it is."

"Thieves like him give all lawyers a bad name."

"Yes, but what will we do?"

"We'll have to call the police and report what we saw."

"You're right. We are not only citizens but, as lawyers, officers of the court too. We have witnessed a murder. We have to call the authorities and report what we have witnessed."

"Did you get a good look at the men?"

"Yes."

"I did too."

"Well then, let's get on with it and call the police."

~~~~~~~~~~~~~~~~~~~~~~~~~~

Colored lights from four police cars flashed as yellow tape was put around the area of the crowded underground garage.

A detective with a notebook approached the two witnesses. "Can you tell us what you saw?" asked the detective of the first lawyer.

"I saw two men stomping the victim. I shouted at them. Then they ran away."

"Can you describe the two men?"

"Yes. One was a white male, short, about five-six, and chubby. The other was a white male, six-two, must have weighed over 200 pounds."

"How would you describe the two men," he asked the second witness.

Robbers

"I'd say the short one was five-five and the tall man was six-three".

TABLOIDS AT THE
CHECKOUT COUNTER

It was Friday afternoon. Jane and Sally were shopping at Wayman's Supermarket across from the park. Each had half-filled her cart with lettuce, bananas, flour and a dozen other items and were in line at the checkout counter. A customer before them had a cart loaded with more than Jane and Sally's combined.

To their right was candy and gum; to their left magazines and tabloid "newspapers." The tabloids caught their attention.

"Jane, can you believe this: 'Man in Tacoma, Washington, Has Skin Like an Alligator.'"

"Not likely. Here's another one: 'Man from Arizona Has Breakfast with Green Men in Flying Saucer.'"

"Look at this, side by side, two of them report Elvis Presley sightings, one in Cincinnati at Meyer's Wine Cellar and one in New York at Radio City Music Hall."

"Hmm," said Jane, "It sounds unlikely. But look at this one: 'Boy Born with Three Heads.'"

"Hey read some more of that one."

"'Noted scientist says it is not one boy with three heads but three boys with one body. Controversy continues,'" read Jane.

"Wow, how ridiculous can you get. Here's another: 'Man Puts Fire Out With Gasoline,'" read Sally.

"I found one that beats yours," said Jane. "Listen to this: 'Three-Year-Old Beats Olympic Gold Medalist in Race Across Pool. Witness said the tyke moved his arms so fast he threw most of the water out of the swimming pool.'"

The woman ahead had paid her bill and was pushing her cart toward the door. Two other customers had gotten in line behind Jane and Sally. The checker looked toward them in readiness, but Sally was so caught up with another headline that she held up her right hand like a traffic cop and held up the paper with her left hand for all to see as she said loudly, "Stop everything and cast your eyes at the mother of all absurdities."

Jane gasped as Sally read: " 'PROFESSOR SAYS, GOVERNMENT CAN SOLVE OUR PROBLEMS.' "

PROMISES, PROMISES

The five leading candidates for the nomination for President of the United States had been invited to a public forum at prestigious Bovundy University. All had accepted.

Marvin Green was one of several students eager to speak. His mother and father had that rare combination of intellectual interests and common sense. Therefore Marvin was educated before enrolling at Bovundy. His character was sufficient to withstand the pressures from the ignorant, prejudiced and hostile professors and teaching assistants who dominated the great university.

Sam Mingella was on the staff of the university. As holder of a master's degree in political science, he thought it appropriate that he was selected to screen the students wanting to question the illustrious guests. Interested students lined up to get on his list.

Carl Charbonnet

Sam would ask each aspiring questioner what question he had for the candidates - then make notes on a clipboard. Marvin's answer was: "I shall ask them why none of them has ever mentioned the most important issue of our age: whether we should have a society planned, organized and directed by the force of government or a society planned, organized and directed voluntarily in peace."

Sam Mingella paused. He thought, *I wonder what he's talking about?* To Marvin he said, "Thank you, Mr. Green. I will call you," as he wrote on his clip board, "Marvin Green - NO."

Marvin was skeptical about his being called, yet he optimistically stayed within the group of students near the microphone.

The forum began. Each candidate was allotted eight minutes to give remarks. Harvey Sault promised to move the country forward into the future. Beth Tilson promised to increase Medicaid payments to the needy. Paul Bristone said if elected, he would increase student loans and grants. Shirley McBain told of her efforts to increase spending for the Department of Education. Malcom Tenderthor said the government should demonstrate that they care for the American people by solving more of their problems.. Then the questions began.

The first student asked if they would promise to pay the complete costs of college, including a stipend for spending money, instead of just most of it like they do now.

The second student asked the panel how they would ensure that giant corporations would stop exploiting the people.

The third student pointed out that one study showed self-esteem was established by age three, and wanted to know what each candidate would do to help three-year-olds build self-esteem.

The fourth student pleaded that the government increase funds for the school-lunch program.

The fifth student asked how they could ensure that people in Rwanda not starve.

Sam Mingella had controlled the students very well and things were working smoothly. But the night before he had eaten thirty-nine ripe persimmons. Now an urgency overcame him just as a friend was passing by. Sam grabbed his friend firmly on his arm with one hand and handed him the clipboard with the other. "Frank," he said, "I have to leave. Take over." Without waiting for a response, he ran out of the auditorium and down the hall.

Marvin noticed the new man's bewilderment and seized the opportunity. He stepped forward with confidence and said, "I'm Marvin Green. It's my turn next." Frank handed him the microphone.

Marvin Green took the microphone and looked at the head table of candidates. "All five of you have

Carl Charbonnet

said what you would do for us, how you would solve our problems."

He gestured around the room at large and said, "Each of the five students who spoke before me has appealed to you to increase governmental intervention into our lives, ostensibly to solve one problem or the other. I say that all the Presidential candidates and all the students have been wrong, 180 degrees, absolutely wrong.

"The proper purpose of government, in my view, is to establish a free and just society so that we might solve our own problems in peace. The Constitution has established for us a limited government. Everything said tonight before I began had as its premise that the Constitution is wrong. Each speaker was interested in engaging the government to solve more problems. Everyone who spoke before me demonstrated their belief in the myth that the government can solve our problems. Everyone who spoke before me is therefore in contravention to the lessons of history and to the Constitution. History has shown that statism - socialism, Liberalism or whatever you call it - is the worst mistake of history, that most of the crimes throughout history as well as today have been committed by governments. All history shows the failure of what every other speaker tonight has endorsed.

"Therefore it is my opinion that the best thing an

Promises, Promises

American can do for his country when a politician promises to solve his problems is to find someone else to vote for.

"Since the Department of Education is illegal – intervening in education is not one of the enumerated rights granted by the Constitution to the national government - and since it is well established that governmental intervention into education has dumbed down reading and math, has stolen our history, and has twisted a knife into the heart of our culture - is there one among you who will, without equivocation, advocate to totally eliminate the Department of Education and to replace it with nothing?"